- Cited by the Guinness Book of World Records as the #1 best-selling writer of all time!

- Author of more than 150 clever, authentic, and sophisticated mystery novels!

- Creator of the amazing Perry Mason, the savvy Della Street, and dynamite detective Paul Drake!

- **THE ONLY AUTHOR WHO OUTSELLS AGATHA CHRISTIE, HAROLD ROBBINS, BARBARA CARTLAND, AND LOUIS L'AMOUR *COMBINED!***

Why?

Because he writes the best, most fascinating whodunits of all!

You'll want to read every one of them, coming soon from
BALLANTINE BOOKS

By Erle Stanley Gardner
Published by Ballantine Books:

The Case of the
Velvet Claws

Erle Stanley Gardner

BALLANTINE BOOKS • NEW YORK

Copyright © 1945 by Erle Stanley Gardner
Copyright renewed 1960 by Erle Stanley Gardner

All rights reserved under International and Pan-American Copyright Conventions. Published in the United States by Ballantine Books, a division of Random House, Inc., New York, and simultaneously in Canada by Random House of Canada Limited, Toronto.

http://www.randomhouse.com

Library of Congress Catalog Card Number: 95-94904

ISBN 0-345-32317-3

Originally published by William Morrow & Co. in 1933.

Manufactured in the United States of America

First Ballantine Books Edition: August 1985

10   9   8

CAST OF CHARACTERS

1

AUTUMN SUN BEAT AGAINST THE WINDOW.

Perry Mason sat at the big desk. There was about him the attitude of one who is waiting. His face in repose was like the face of a chess player who is studying the board. That face seldom changed expression. Only the eyes changed expression. He gave the impression of being a thinker and a fighter, a man who could work with infinite patience to jockey an adversary into just the right position, and then finish him with one terrific punch.

Book cases, filled with leather-backed books, lined the walls of the room. A big safe was in one corner. There were two chairs, in addition to the swivel chair which Perry Mason occupied. The office held an atmosphere of plain, rugged efficiency, as though it had absorbed something of the personality of the man who occupied it.

The door to the outer office opened, and Della Street, his secretary, eased her way into the room and closed the door behind her.

"A woman," she said, "who claims to be a Mrs. Eva Griffin."

Perry Mason looked at the girl with level eyes.

"And you don't think she is?" he asked.

She shook her head.

"She looks phony to me," she said. "I've looked up the Griffins in the telephone book. And there isn't any Griffin who has an address like the one she gave. I looked in the City Directory, and got the same result. There are a lot of Griffins, but I don't find any Eva Griffin. And I don't find any at her address."

"What was the address?" asked Mason.

"2271 Grove Street," she said.

Perry Mason made a notation on a slip of paper.

"I'll see her," he said.

"Okay," said Della Street. "I just wanted you to know that she looks phony to me."

Della Street was slim of figure, steady of eye; a young woman of approximately twenty-seven, who gave the impression of watching life with keenly appreciative eyes and seeing far below the surface.

She remained standing in the doorway eyeing Perry Mason with quiet insistence. "I wish," she said, "that you'd find out who she really is before we do anything for her."

"A hunch?" asked Perry Mason.

"You might call it that," she said, smiling.

Perry Mason nodded. His face had not changed expression. Only his eyes had become warily watchful.

"All right, send her in, and I'll take a look at her myself."

Della Street closed the door as she went out, keeping a hand on the knob, however. Within a few seconds, the knob turned, the door opened, and a woman walked into the room with an air of easy assurance.

She was in her early thirties, or perhaps, her late twenties—well groomed, and giving an appearance of being exceedingly well cared for. She flashed a swiftly appraising glance about the office before she looked at the man seated behind the desk.

"Come in and sit down," said Perry Mason.

She looked at him then, and there was a faint expression of annoyance upon her face. It was as though she expected men to get up when she came into the room, and to treat her with a deferential recognition of her sex and her position.

2

For just a moment she seemed inclined to ignore his invitation. Then she walked to the chair across from the desk, sat down in it, and looked at Perry Mason.

"Well?" he asked.

"You're Mr. Mason, the attorney?"

"Yes."

The blue eyes which had been looking at him in cautious appraisal, suddenly widened as though by an effort. They gave to her face an expression of utter innocence.

"I am in trouble," she said.

Perry Mason nodded as though the news meant nothing to him, other than a matter of daily routine.

When she didn't go on, he said: "Most people who come in here are."

The woman said, abruptly: "You don't make it easy for me to tell you about it. Most of the attorneys I have consulted . . ."

She was suddenly silent.

Perry Mason smiled at her. Slowly he got to his feet, put his hands on the edge of the desk and leaned his weight on them so that his body was leaning toward her across the desk. "Yes," he said, "I know. Most of the attorneys that you've consulted have had expensive suites of offices and a lot of clerks running in and out. You've paid them big money and haven't had anything much to show for it. They've bowed and scraped when you came in the room, and charged you big retainers. But when you get in a real jam you don't dare to go to them."

Her wide eyes narrowed somewhat. For two or three seconds they stared at each other, and then the woman lowered her eyes.

Perry Mason continued to speak, slowly and forcefully, yet without raising his voice.

"All right," he said, "I'm different. I get my business because I fight for it, and because I fight for my clients. Nobody ever called on me to organize a corporation, and I've never yet probated an estate. I haven't drawn up

3

over a dozen contracts in my life, and I wouldn't know how to go about foreclosing a mortgage. People that come to me don't come to me because they like the looks of my eyes, or the way my office is furnished, or because they've known me at a club. They come to me because they need me. They come to me because they want to hire me for what I can do."

She looked up at him then. "Just what is it that you do, Mr. Mason?" she asked.

He snapped out two words at her. "I fight!"

She nodded vigorously. "That's exactly what I want you to do for me."

He sat down again in his swivel chair, and lit a cigarette. The atmosphere seemed to have been cleared as though the two personalities had created an electrical storm which had subsided. "All right," he said. "Now we've wasted enough time with preliminaries. Get down to earth, and tell me what it is you want. Tell me first who you are and how you happened to come to me. Maybe it'll make it easier for you if you start in that way."

She began to speak rapidly, as though she had rehearsed what she was saying.

"I am married. My name is Eva Griffin, and I reside at 2271 Grove Street. I have trouble that I can't very well discuss with the attorneys who have heretofore represented me. A friend who asked her name withheld, told me about you. She said that you were more than a lawyer. That you went out and did things."

She was silent for a moment, and then asked: "Is it true?"

Perry Mason nodded his head.

"I suppose so," he said. "Most attorneys hire clerks and detectives to work up their cases, and find out about the evidence. I don't, for the simple reason that I can't trust any one to do that sort of stuff in the kind of cases I handle. I don't handle very many, but when I do I'm

4

well paid, and I usually give good results. When I hire a detective, he's hired to get just one fact."

She nodded quickly and eagerly. Now that the ice was broken, she seemed eager to go on with her story.

"You read in the paper about the hold-up at the Beechwood Inn last night? There were some guests, you know, in the main dining room, and some in the private dining rooms. A man tried to hold up the guests, and somebody shot him."

Perry Mason nodded. "I read about it," he said.

"I was there."

He shrugged his shoulders. "Know anything about who did the shooting?"

She lowered her eyes for a moment, and then raised them to his. "No," she said.

He looked at her, narrowed his eyes and scowled.

She met the stare for a second or two, then lowered her eyes.

Perry Mason continued to wait as though she had not answered his question.

After a moment she raised her eyes once more, and fidgeted uneasily in the chair. "Well," she said, "if you're going to be my attorney, I should tell you the truth. Yes."

Mason's nod seemed more of satisfaction than affirmation.

"Go on," he told her.

"We tried to get out, and couldn't. The entrances were all watched. It seems somebody had put through a call to the police department before the shooting, just when the hold-up started. Before we could get out, the police had the place sewed up."

"Who is 'we'?" he asked.

She studied the tip of her shoe, then said in a mumbled voice: "Harrison Burke."

Perry Mason said, slowly: "You mean Harrison Burke, the one who's candidate for . . ."

"Yes," she snapped, as though she would interrupt

him before he could say anything concerning Harrison Burke.

"What were you doing there with him?"

"Dining and dancing."

"Well?" he inquired.

"Well," she said, "we went back into the private dining room, and kept out of sight until the officers started taking the names of the witnesses. The sergeant in charge was a friend of Harrison's, and he knew that it would be fatal for the newspapers to get hold of the fact that we were there. So he let us stay on in the dining room until after everything was finished, and then he smuggled us out of the back door."

"Anybody see you?" asked Mason.

She shook her head. "Nobody that I know."

"All right," he said, "go on from there."

She looked up at him and said, abruptly: "Do you know Frank Locke?"

He nodded his head. "You mean the one that edits *Spicy Bits*?"

She clamped her lips together in a firm line, and nodded her head in silent assent.

"What about him?" asked Perry Mason.

"He knows about it," she said.

"Going to publish it?" he asked.

She nodded.

Perry Mason fingered a paper weight on his desk. His hand was well formed, long and tapering, yet the fingers seemed filled with competent strength. It seemed the hand could have a grip of crushing force should the occasion require.

"You can buy him off," he said.

"No," she said, "I can't. You've got to."

"Why can't Harrison Burke?" he asked.

"Don't you understand?" she said. "Harrison Burke might explain his having been at the Beechwood Inn with a married woman. But he could never explain paying hush

6

money to silence a scandal sheet from publishing the fact. He's got to keep out of this. They may trap him."

Perry Mason drummed with his fingers on the top of the desk.

"And you want me to square the thing?" he asked.

"I want you to square it."

"How high would you pay?"

She rushed on in swift conversation now, leaning toward him and talking rapidly.

"Listen," she said, "I'm going to tell you something. Remember what it is, but don't ask me how I happened to know. I don't think you can buy Frank Locke off. You've got to go higher. Frank Locke pretends to own *Spicy Bits*. You know the kind of a publication it is. It's just a blackmailing sheet, and that's all it's for. They are in the market for all they can get. But Frank Locke is only a figurehead. There's somebody behind him. Somebody who is higher. Somebody who really owns the paper. They've got a good attorney who tries to keep them clear of blackmailing charges and libel suits. But in case anything ever went wrong, Frank Locke is there to take all the blame."

She quit talking.

There was a moment or two of silence.

"I'm listening," said Perry Mason.

She bit her lip for a moment, then raised her eyes once more, and continued speaking in the same rapid tone. "They've found out about Harrison being there. They don't know who the woman was that was with him. But they're going to publish the fact that he was there, and demand that the police bring him in as a witness. There's some mystery about the shooting. It looks as though some one had trapped this man into a hold-up so that he could be shot, without too many questions being asked. The police and the District Attorney are going to grill every one who was there."

7

"And they're not going to grill you?" asked Perry Mason.

She shook her head. "No, they're going to leave us out of it. Nobody knows I was there. The officer knows Harrison was there. That's all. I gave him an assumed name."

"Well?" asked Mason.

"Don't you see?" she said. "If they put pressure to bear on the officers, they'll have to question Harrison. And then he'll have to tell them who the woman was that was with him. Or else it will appear worse than it really was. As a matter of fact, there wasn't anything wrong with it. We had a right to be there."

He drummed with his fingers on his desk for a few moments, and then looked at her steadily.

"All right," he said, "let's not have any misunderstanding about this. You're trying to save Harrison Burke's political career?"

She looked at him meaningly.

"No," she said. "*I* don't want any misunderstanding about it. I'm trying to save myself."

He continued to drum with his fingertips for a few minutes, and then said: "It's going to take money."

She opened her handbag. "I came prepared for that."

Perry Mason watched her while she counted out the currency, and arranged it in piles along the edge of the desk.

"What's that?" he asked.

"That's on account of your fee," she said. "When you find out how much it's going to take to keep the thing secret, you can get in touch with me."

"How do I get in touch with you?"

"You put a personal in the *Examiner:* 'E. G. Negotiations ready to conclude,' and you sign that with your initials. Then I'll come to your office."

"I don't like it," he said. "I never like to pay blackmail. I'd rather work some other way around it."

"What other way would there be?" she asked.

8

He shrugged his shoulders. "I don't know. Sometimes there are other ways."

She said, hopefully: "I can tell you one thing about Frank Locke. There's something in his past life that he's afraid of. I don't know exactly what it is. I think perhaps he was sent to prison once, or something of that sort."

He looked at her.

"You seem to know him pretty well."

She shook her head. "I never saw him in my life."

"How do you know so much about him?"

"I told you you weren't to ask me that."

He drummed again with his powerful fingers on the edge of the desk.

"Can I say that I am representing Harrison Burke?" he asked.

She shook her head emphatically.

"You can't say that you're representing anybody. That is, you can't use any names. You know how to handle that. I don't."

"When do you want me to start in?"

"Right away."

Perry Mason pressed a button on the side of his desk. After a moment or two, the door to the outer office opened and Della Street came in carrying a notebook.

The woman in the chair sat back with a detached, impersonal air; the manner of one whose business is not to be discussed in any way before servants.

"You wanted something?" asked Della Street.

Perry Mason reached in the upper right-hand drawer of his desk, and took out a letter.

"This letter," he said, "is all right, with the exception of one thing that I want in it. I'll write that in in pen and ink. And then you can re-type the letter. I'm going to be out on important business for the rest of the day. And I don't know just when I'll be back to the office."

Della Street asked: "Can I get in touch with you anywhere?"

He shook his head. "I'll get in touch with you," he said.

He drew the letter toward him and scribbled on the margin. She hesitated for a moment, then walked around the desk so that she could look over his shoulder.

Perry Mason wrote on the letter: "Go back to the outer office. Ring Drake's Detective Bureau, and ask for Paul Drake. Get him to shadow this woman when she leaves the office. But don't let her know she's being tailed. Tell him I want to find out who she is, that it's important."

He took a blotter, blotted the note, and handed it to Della Street.

"Have that attended to right away," he said, "so that I can sign it before I go out."

She took the letter casually. "Very well," she said, and left the office.

Perry Mason turned to the woman. "I've got to know something about how high I can go on this thing," he told her.

"What would you consider reasonable?" she asked.

"Nothing at all," he said crisply. "I don't like to pay money for blackmail."

"I know," she remarked, "but you must have had *some* experience."

"*Spicy Bits,*" he told her, "will charge everything they think the traffic will bear. What I'm trying to get at is, how much will it bear? If they want too much I'll try stalling them along. If they are willing to be reasonable, I can handle it quickly."

"You've *got* to handle it quickly."

"Well," he said, "we're getting away from the question. How much?"

"I could raise five thousand dollars," she ventured.

"Harrison Burke is in politics," he told her. "From all I can hear, he isn't in politics for his health. He runs with the reform crowd, and that makes his patronage all the more valuable to the other crowd."

10

"What are you getting at?" she asked him.

"I'm getting at the fact that *Spicy Bits* probably won't consider five thousand a drop in the bucket."

"I *could* raise nine or perhaps ten," she said, "in a pinch."

"It'll be a pinch," he told her.

She bit her lower lip between her teeth.

"Suppose something turns up and I need to communicate with you without waiting for the ad to be published in the paper?" he asked. "Where can I get in touch with you?"

She shook her head swiftly and positively.

"You can't. That's one thing that we've got to have understood. Don't try to reach me at my address. Don't try to telephone me. Don't try to find out who my husband is."

"You're living with your husband?"

She snapped him a swift look.

"Of course I am, otherwise where would I get the money?"

There was a knock at the outer door of the office, and Della Street thrust her head and shoulders into the room.

"I have that matter attended to so you can sign the letter any time you want, Mr. Mason," she said.

Perry Mason got to his feet, looked meaningly at the woman.

"All right, Mrs. Griffin. I'll do the best I can."

She arose from her chair, took a step toward the door, paused, and looked at the money on the table.

"Do I get a receipt for the money?" she asked.

"You do if you want it."

"I think I would like to have it."

"Of course," he said, meaningly, "if you would like to have in your purse, a receipt made out to Eva Griffin for a retainer, and signed by Perry Mason, it's quite all right with me."

She frowned, and then said: "Don't make it that way.

11

Make a receipt to the effect that the holder of this receipt has paid you the amount mentioned, as a retainer."

He scowled, scooped up the money with his swiftly competent hands, and beckoned to Della Street.

"Here, Della," he said, "take this money. Give Mrs. Griffin a ledger page, and make a receipt to the effect that the account listed in our ledger, under that page number, is credited with five hundred dollars. Mark on the receipt that that amount is by way of retainer."

"Can you tell me what your total fees will be?" asked the woman.

"It'll depend on the amount of the work," he said. "They'll be high, but fair. And they'll depend on results."

She nodded, hesitated a moment, and then said: "I guess that's all I have to do in here."

"My secretary will give you the receipt," he told her.

She smiled at him. "Good day."

"Good day," he said.

She paused at the door of the outer office, to turn and look back at him.

He was standing with his back to her, his hands thrust in his pockets, looking out of the window.

"This way, please," said Della Street, and closed the door.

Perry Mason continued to stare out at the street for some five minutes. Then the door from the outer office opened once more, and Della Street came into the office.

"She's gone," she said.

Mason whirled to face her.

"Why did you think she was phony?" he asked.

Della Street stared him steadily in the eye.

"That woman," she said, "spells trouble to me."

He shrugged his broad shoulders.

"To me, she's five hundred dollars cash for a retainer. And another fifteen hundred by way of a fee when I get the thing squared up."

The girl said, with some feeling: "She's phony, and

12

she's crooked. She's one of those well-kept little minxes that would double-cross anybody in order to take care of herself."

Perry Mason surveyed her appraisingly.

"You don't find loyalty in wives," he said, "who pay five hundred dollar retainers. She's a client."

Della Street shook her head, and said: "That isn't what I meant. I meant that there's something false about her. She's concealing something from you right now; something that you should know. She's sending you up against something as a blind proposition when she could make it easy for you if she'd only be frank."

Perry Mason made a gesture with his shoulders.

"Why should I care if she makes it easy for me?" he asked. "She's the one that's paying for my time. Time is all I'm investing."

Della Street said, slowly: "Are you sure that time is all you're investing?"

"Why not?"

"I don't know," she said, "the woman's dangerous. She is just the kind of a little minx who would get you into some sort of a jam and leave you to take it, right on the button."

His face didn't change expression, but his eyes glinted. "That's one of the chances I have to take," he told her. "I can't expect my clients to be loyal to me. They pay me money. That's all."

She stared at him with a speculative look that held something of a wistful tenderness. "But you insist on being loyal to your clients, no matter how rotten they are."

"Of course," he told her. "That's my duty."

"To your profession?"

"No," he said slowly, "to myself. I'm a paid gladiator. I fight for my clients. Most clients aren't square shooters. That's why they're clients. They've got themselves into trouble. It's up to me to get them out. I have to shoot

13

square with them. I can't always expect them to shoot square with me."

"It isn't fair!" she blazed.

"Of course not," he smiled. "It's business."

She shrugged her shoulders. "I told the detective that you wanted her shadowed as soon as she left the office," she said, abruptly getting back to her duties. "He said he'd be there to pick her up."

"You talked with Paul Drake himself?"

"Of course, otherwise I wouldn't have told you everything was all right."

"Okay," he said, "you can bank three hundred out of that retainer, and give me two hundred to put in my pocket. We'll find out who she really is, and then we'll have an ace in the hole."

Della Street went back to the outer office, returned with two hundred dollars in currency, which she handed to Perry Mason.

He smiled at her.

"You're a good girl, Della," he said. "Even if you do get funny ideas about women."

She whirled on him. "I *hate* her!" she said, "I hate the very ground she walks on! But it isn't that. It's something more than the hate. It's sort of a hunch I've got."

He planted his feet wide apart, thrust his hands in his pockets, and stared at her.

"Why do you hate her?" he asked, with tolerant amusement.

"I hate everything she stands for!" said Della Street. "I've had to work for everything I got. I never got a thing in life that I didn't work for. And lots of times I've worked for things and have had nothing in return. That woman is the type that has never worked for anything in her life! She doesn't give a damned thing in return for what she gets. Not even herself."

Perry Mason pursed his lips thoughtfully. "And all of this outburst is occasioned just because you gave her the

14

once-over and didn't like the way she was dressed?" he asked.

"I liked the way she was dressed. She's dressed like a million dollars. Those clothes she had on cost somebody a lot of money. And you can bet that she wasn't the one that paid for them. She's *too* well-kept, *too* well-groomed, *too* baby faced. Did you notice that trick she has of making her eyes wide when she wants to impress you? She's practiced that baby stare in front of a mirror."

He watched her with eyes that were suddenly deep and enigmatical. "If all clients had your loyalty, Della, there wouldn't be any law business. Don't forget that. You've got to take clients as they come. You're different. Your family was rich. Then they lost their money. You went to work. Lots of women wouldn't have done that."

Her eyes were wistful once more.

"What would they have done?" she asked. "What could they have done?"

"They could," he remarked slowly, "have married a man, and then gone out to the Beechwood Inn with some other man, got caught, and had to get a lawyer to get them out of the jam."

She turned toward the outer office, keeping her eyes averted from him. Those eyes were glowing. "I started to talk about clients," she observed, "and you begin to talk about me." And she pushed her way through the door and into the outer office.

Perry Mason walked to the doorway and stood there while Della Street went over to her desk, sat down at it, and slid a sheet of paper into her typewriter. Mason was still standing there when the door of the outer office opened and a tall man, with drooping shoulders and a head that was thrust forward on a long neck, came into the outer office. He regarded Della Street with protruding glassy eyes that held a perpetual expression of droll humor, smiled at her, turned to Mason and said: "Hello, Perry."

15

Mason said: "Come on in, Paul. Did you get anything?"

Drake said: "I got back."

Mason held the door open, and closed it after the detective had gone into the private office.

"What happened?" he asked.

Paul Drake sat down in the chair which the woman had occupied a few minutes earlier, raised his foot to the other chair and lit a cigarette.

"She's a wise baby," he said.

"What makes you think so?" asked Perry Mason. "Did she know you were tailing her?"

"I don't think so," said Drake. "I stood by the elevator shaft, where I could see her when she came out of the office. When she came out, I got in the elevator first. She kept watching your office to see if anybody came out of it. I think she thought perhaps you'd send your girl to try and spot her. She seemed relieved when the elevator got down.

"She walked to the corner, and I tagged along behind, keeping a few people between her and me. She ducked into the department store across the street, walked right along as though she knew exactly what she wanted to do, and went into the Women's Rest Room.

"She looked sort of funny when she went in there, and I had an idea maybe it was a dodge, so I hunted up an attendant, and asked him if there was any other way out of the Women's Rest Room. It seems there are three ways out. There's a way that goes into the beauty parlor. There's a way into the manicuring room, and a way into the café."

"Which way did she take?" asked Mason.

"She took the beauty parlor just about fifteen seconds before I covered it. I figured she'd simply used the dressing room stuff as a blind. She knew that a man couldn't follow her in there, and she'd evidently figured it all out in advance. I found out this much, she had a car parked in front of the beauty parlor street exit, with a chauffeur

16

sitting at the wheel. The car was a big Lincoln, if that'll help you any."

"It won't," said Mason.

"I didn't think it would," grinned Drake.

2

■

FRANK LOCKE HAD COARSE, MAHOGANY SKIN, AND WORE a tweed suit. His skin didn't have the tanned appearance which comes from outdoor sports, but looked rather as though it had absorbed so much nicotine that it had become stained. His eyes were a mild brown, the color of milk chocolate, and absolutely without sheen. They seemed dead and lifeless. His nose was big, and his mouth weak. To a casual observer, he seemed utterly mild and innocuous.

"Well," he said, "you can talk here."

Perry Mason shook his head. "No, you've got this place rigged up with all sorts of dictographs. I'll talk where I know that you're the only one that'll hear what I'm going to say."

"Where?" asked Frank Locke.

"You can come to my office," said Mason, without hope or enthusiasm in his tone.

Frank Locke laughed, and his laugh was gratingly mirthless.

"Now I'll tell one," he said.

"Okay," said Mason. "Put on your hat, and start out with me. We'll agree on some place."

"How do you mean?" asked Locke, his eyes suddenly suspicious.

"We'll pick a hotel," said Mason.

"One that you've picked out already?" asked Locke.

"No," said Mason, "we'll get a cab and tell him to drive us around. If you're that suspicious, you can pick the hotel yourself."

Frank Locke hesitated a minute, then said: "Excuse me a moment. I'll have to see if it's all right for me to leave the office. I've got some things that I've been working on."

"Okay," said Mason, and sat down.

Frank Locke jumped up from behind the desk and left the room. He left the door open as he went out. From the outer offices came the clack of busy typewriters, the hum of voices. Perry Mason sat and smoked placidly. His face held that expression of absorbed concentration which was so typical of him.

He waited almost ten minutes. Then Frank Locke came in, wearing his hat.

"All right," he said, "I can leave now."

The two men left the building together, hailed a cruising cab.

"Drive around the business section," said Perry Mason.

Locke regarded the attorney with those chocolate brown eyes of his, which seemed to contain no expression whatever.

"Maybe we could talk here," he said.

Mason shook his head. "I want to talk where I don't have to yell."

Locke grinned and said: "I'm used to being yelled at."

Mason said, grimly: "When I yell, I mean business."

Locke lit a cigarette, with a bored air.

"Yeah?" he said casually.

The cab turned to the left. "There's a hotel," said Mason.

Locke grinned. "I see it," he said. "I don't like it because you picked it out, and because it's too near. I'm going to pick the hotel."

Perry Mason said: "Okay. Go ahead and pick one. Just don't tell the driver where to go. Let him drive around and you can pick any hotel that he drives by."

Locke laughed. "Getting cautious, ain't we?"

Perry Mason nodded.

Locke tapped on the glass. "We'll get out here," he said, "at the hotel."

The cab driver looked at him with mild surprise but braked the car to a stop. Mason flipped him a fifty cent piece, and the two men walked into the lobby of the cheap hotel.

"How about the parlor?" asked Locke.

"Suits me," said Mason.

They walked across the lobby, took the elevator to the mezzanine floor, walked past the manicurist's room, and sat down in chairs that faced each other, with a smoking stand in between.

"All right," said Locke, "you're Perry Mason, an attorney. You're representing somebody, and you want something. Shoot!"

Mason said: "I want something kept out of your paper."

"Lots of people do," said Locke. "What do you want out?"

Mason said: "Well, let's discuss procedure first. Are you willing to talk a straight money proposition?"

Locke shook his head emphatically.

"We're not a blackmailing sheet," he said. "We sometimes extend favors to our advertisers."

"Oh, that's it, is it?" said Mason.

"That's it," said Locke.

"What would I advertise?" asked Mason.

Locke shrugged his shoulders. "We don't care," he said, "you don't need to advertise anything, if you don't want to. We sell you the space. That's all."

"I see," said Mason.

"Okay. What is it you want?"

"There was a murder at the Beechwood Inn last night. That is, there was a shooting. I don't know whether it was a murder or not. I understand that the man who was shot was trying to hold up the joint."

Frank Locke turned his dispassionate milk-chocolate eyes upon the attorney.

"Well?" he asked.

Mason continued: "I understand there's some mystery about the thing. That is, the District Attorney is going to make quite an investigation."

Locke said: "You still haven't told me anything."

"I'm telling you," said Mason.

"Okay. Go ahead."

"Somebody told me," continued Mason, "that the list of witnesses that was handed to the District Attorney might not be complete."

Locke stared at him.

"Who do you represent?" he asked.

"A possible advertiser in your paper," said Mason.

"All right. Go on. Let's hear the rest of it," Locke invited.

"You know the rest of it," said Mason.

"Even if I did, I wouldn't admit it," Locke replied. "I don't do anything except sell advertising space. *You've* got to come out in the open. You're the one that comes all the way. I don't budge an inch."

"Okay," Mason said. "As an advertiser in your paper, I wouldn't like to see it mix into that murder too closely. That is, I wouldn't like to have it mention the name of any witness who might have been there, but whose name wasn't included on the list which was given to the District Attorney. I would particularly dislike to see your paper come out with the name of some prominent witness whose name had been omitted from that list, and ask why he was not summoned as a witness and questioned. And, still

20

speaking as an advertiser, I would dislike very much to see any comment made in any way about this witness having a companion with him, or any surmises as to the identity of that companion. Now then, how much is advertising space going to cost me?"

"Well," said Locke, "if you're going to dictate the policies of the paper, you'll have to take quite a bit of advertising. It would have to be handled under a contract. I would draw up an advertising contract with you, and agree to sell you the space over a period of time. The agreement would contain a clause for liquidated damages in the event you broke the contract. Then, if you didn't want to take all the advertising, you could pay over the sum of liquidated damages."

Perry Mason said: "I could pay over that sum just as soon as I broke the contract?"

"Sure," said Locke.

"And I could break the contract just as soon as it was drawn up, eh?"

"No," said Locke. "We wouldn't like that. You'd have to wait a day or two."

"There'd be no action taken while I was waiting, of course," said Mason.

"Of course."

Mason took out a cigarette case, fished out a cigarette with his long, capable fingers, lit it, and surveyed Locke with eyes that were cold and uncordial.

"All right," he said. "I've said everything I came to say. Now I'm listening."

Locke got up from his chair and took several paces up and down the floor. His head was thrust forward, and his chocolate colored eyes blinked rapidly.

"I've got to think this thing over," he said.

Mason took out his watch and looked at it. "All right, you've got ten minutes to do your thinking in."

"No, no," said Locke. "It's going to take a little while to think it over."

"No, it isn't," said Mason.

"I say it is."

"You've got ten minutes," insisted Mason.

"You're the one that came to me," said Locke. "I didn't come to you."

Mason said: "Don't be foolish. Remember that I'm representing a client. You've got to make a proposition to me, and I've got to see that it's transmitted to my client. And it isn't going to be easy to get in touch with that client."

Locke raised his eyebrows. "Like that, eh?" he said.

"Like that," said Mason.

Locke said: "Well, maybe I could think it over in ten minutes. But I've got to call the office."

"Okay," said Mason. "Go ahead and call your office. I'll wait right here."

Locke went at once to the elevator and went down to the main floor. Mason strolled to the railing of the mezzanine and watched him cross the lobby. Locke did not go to the telephone booths, but left the hotel.

Mason went to the elevators, pressed the button, went down to the lobby, straight through the door, and crossed the street. He stood in a doorway, smoking and watching the buildings across the street.

After three or four minutes, Locke came out of a drug store and walked into the hotel.

Mason crossed the street, entered the hotel a few steps behind Locke, and followed him until he came abreast of the telephone booths. Then Mason stepped into one of the telephone booths, left the door open, thrust out his head and called: "Oh, Locke."

Locke whirled, his chocolate brown eyes suddenly wide with alarm, and stared at Mason.

"Got to thinking," explained Mason, "that I'd better telephone and see if I could get in touch with my client. So that I could give you an immediate answer. But I can't get a call through. Nobody answers. I'm waiting to get my money back."

Locke nodded. His eyes were still suspicious.

"Let the money go," he said. "Our time's worth more than that."

Mason said: "Maybe yours is," and stepped back to the telephone. He jiggled the receiver two or three times, then shrugged his shoulders with an exclamation of disgust, and left the telephone booth. The two men rode together in the elevator to the mezzanine floor, and returned to the chairs they had occupied.

"Well?" said Mason.

"I've been thinking the thing over," said Frank Locke, and hesitated.

Mason commented, dryly: "Well, I presumed that you had."

"You know," said Locke, "the situation that you've brought up, without mentioning any names, might have a very important political angle."

"Again," said Mason, "still without mentioning any names, it might not. But there's no use you and me sitting here trying to kid each other like a couple of horse traders. What's your price?"

"The advertising contract," said Locke, "would have to have a proviso that in the event it was breached, a payment of twenty thousand dollars would be made as liquidated damages."

"You're crazy!" exclaimed Mason.

Frank Locke shrugged his shoulders. "You're the one that wanted to buy the advertising," he said. "I don't know as I'm anxious to sell it to you."

Mason got to his feet. "You don't act as though you wanted to sell anything," he remarked. He walked to the elevator and Locke followed him.

"Maybe you'll want to buy some advertising again sometime," Locke said. "Our rates are somewhat elastic you know."

"Meaning that they're going down?" queried Mason.

"Meaning that they may go up, in *this* case."

"Oh," said Mason, shortly.

He paused abruptly, and whirled, staring at Locke with cold, hostile eyes.

"Listen," he said. "I know what I'm up against. And I'm telling you right now that you can't get away with it."

"Can't get away with what?" said Locke.

"You know damned well what you can't get away with," said Mason. "By God! You fellows have run a blackmailing sheet here and made people eat out of your hands long enough. I'm telling you right now where you head in!"

Locke regained something of his composure, and shrugged his shoulders.

"I've had fellows try to tell me that before," he said.

"I didn't say I was *trying* to tell you," said Mason. "I said I was *telling* you."

"And I heard you," said Locke. "There's no need of raising your voice."

"Okay," said Mason. "Just so you know what I mean. By God! I'm starting after you fellows right now."

Locke smiled. "Very well. In the meantime, would you mind pressing the elevator button, or else get out of the way, so that I can press it."

Mason turned and pressed the button. They rode down in silence, walked across the lobby.

When they reached the street, Locke smiled.

"Well," he said, his brown eyes staring at Perry Mason, "there's no hard feelings."

Perry Mason turned his back.

"The hell there ain't," he said.

3

PERRY MASON SAT IN HIS AUTOMOBILE, AND LIT A CIG-
arette from the butt of the one he had just smoked. His
face was set in lines of patient concentration, his eyes
glittered. He seemed like some pugilist seated in his corner, waiting for the gong to ring. Yet there was no expression of nervousness upon his face. The only thing
which indicated strain was the fact that he had been
lighting cigarettes, one after the other, for more than an
hour.

Directly across the street was the building in which
Spicy Bits had its editorial offices.

Mason was half way through the last cigarette in the
package, when Frank Locke came out of the building.

Locke walked with a furtive manner, glancing about
him mechanically, with eyes that didn't seem to be looking for anything in particular, but were peering, purely as
a matter of habit. His appearance was that of a fox who
has been prowling until after daylight and is caught slink-
ing back to his lair by the rays of the early sun.

Perry Mason flipped away the cigarette and pressed his
foot on the starter. The light coupé slid away from the
curb and into the stream of traffic.

Locke turned to the right at the corner and hailed a
taxicab. Mason trailed the cab closely until traffic thinned
slightly, when he dropped farther behind.

Frank Locke's cab pulled up in front of a neighborhood

bar and grill which seemed deserted except for the bartender. He paid off the driver and stood watching while the cab drove off. Then he shrugged his shoulders and entered the bar and ordered a drink, tossed it off quickly and ordered another.

Perry Mason parked his car half a block away, took out a fresh package of cigarettes, broke the cellophane, and started smoking again.

Frank Locke stayed in the bar about three quarters of an hour. Then he came out, looked quickly about him, and walked to the corner. The alcohol had given him a certain air of assurance, and caused him to throw his shoulders back slightly.

Perry Mason watched while Locke found a cruising cab, and climbed in. Mason trailed along behind the cab until Locke discharged it in front of a hotel. Then he parked his car, went into the hotel lobby, and looked cautiously around him. There was no sign of Locke.

Mason looked the lobby over. The place was a commercial type of hotel, catering to salesmen and conventions. There was a line of telephone booths, with an operator stationed at a desk. Quite a few people were in the lobby.

Perry Mason moved slowly and cautiously about, looking the people over. Then he walked over to the desk.

"Can you tell me," he asked the clerk, "whether or not Frank Locke has a room here?"

The clerk ran his finger down the card index system, and said, "We have a John Lock."

"No," said Mason, "this is Frank Locke."

"He's not with us. Sorry," said the clerk.

"That's all right," said Mason, turning away.

He crossed the lobby to the dining room and looked in there. There were a few people eating at the tables but Locke was not among them. There was a barber shop in the basement, and Mason went down the stairs and peered in through the glass partition.

26

Locke was in the third chair from the end, his face covered with hot towels. Mason recognized him by the tweed suit, and tan shoes.

Mason nodded and went back up the stairs to the lobby. He crossed to the girl at the telephone desk.

"All the booth calls are handled through you?" he asked.

She nodded.

"Okay. I can show you how to pick up twenty dollars pretty easy."

She stared at him, and asked, "Are you kidding me?"

Mason shook his head. "Listen," he said, "I want to get a number, and that's all."

"How do you mean?"

"Just this," he said, "I'm going to put through a call for a man. He probably won't take the call right away, but will come up here to get it later on. He's in the barber shop now. After he talks with me, he's going to call a number. I want to know what that number is."

"But," said the girl, "suppose he doesn't put the call through here?"

"In that case," Mason told her, "you've done the best you can, and you get the twenty bucks anyway."

"I'm not supposed to give out information about those things," the girl protested.

"That's why you're getting twenty bucks for it," Mason said, smiling. "That, and listening in on the call."

"Oh, I couldn't listen in on a call, and tell you what was said."

"You don't have to. *I'll* tell *you* what's said. All I want you to do is check up on it, so as to make sure that the number I get is the number I want."

She hesitated, looked furtively about her as though fearful that some one might know what they were talking about, merely from a casual inspection.

Perry Mason took out two ten dollar bills from his pocket, folded them, and twisted them quietly.

The eyes of the girl dropped to the bills, and remained there.

"Okay," she said, at length.

Mason passed over the twenty dollars.

"The man's name," he told her, "is Locke. I'll call in in about two minutes, and have him paged. Now the conversation will be this. Locke will call a party and ask if it's all right to pay four hundred dollars for information about the name of a woman. The party will tell him it's all right."

The girl nodded her head, slowly.

"Do incoming calls come in through you?" asked Mason.

"No," she said, "not unless you ask for station thirteen."

"All right, I'll ask for station thirteen."

He grinned at her, and went out.

He found a drug store in the next block which had a public telephone. He called the number of the hotel, and asked for station thirteen.

"Okay," he said, when he heard the girl's voice. "I'm calling for Frank Locke. Have him paged and be sure that you tell him to come to your station for the call. He probably won't come now, but I'll hold the line. He's in the barber shop. But don't tell the bellboy that I said he was. Simply tell him to look in the barber shop."

"I getcha," said the girl.

He held the line for some two minutes, and then the girl's voice said, "He said to leave your number, and he'd call you back."

"That's fine," said Mason, "the number is Harrison 23850. But tell the bellboy to be sure that he goes to your station to get the call."

"Sure, don't worry about that."

"All right," said Mason, "tell him to ask for Mr. Smith at that number."

"Any initials?"

"No, just Smith, and the number. That's all."

28

"Okay," she said. "I gotcha."

Mason hung up.

He waited approximately ten minutes, and then the telephone rang.

He answered it in a high-pitched, querulous voice, and heard Locke's voice speaking cautiously at the other end of the wire.

"Listen," said Mason, using the high-pitched voice; "let's not have any misunderstanding about this. You're Frank Locke from *Spicy Bits?*"

"Yes," said Locke. "Who are you, and how did you know where to reach me?"

"I got into the office about two minutes after you'd left, and they told me that I could reach you in a speakeasy out on Webster Street, or later on, here in the hotel."

"How the devil did they know that?" asked Locke.

"I don't know," said Mason. "That's what they told me. That's all."

"Well, what was it you wanted?"

"Listen," said Mason, "I know you don't want to talk business over the telephone. But this has got to be handled fast. You folks aren't in business for your health. I know that, the same as everybody else does. And I ain't in business for my health either."

"Listen," Locke's voice was cautious. "I don't know who you are, but you'd better come and see me personally. How far are you from the hotel here?"

Mason said, "I'm nowheres near the hotel. Now listen, I can give you something that's valuable to you. I won't give it out over the telephone, and, if you don't want it, I've got another market for the information. All I want to know is whether or not you're interested. Would you like to find out the name of the woman that was with Harrison Burke last night?"

There was silence over the telephone for some four or five seconds.

"We're a publication that deals with spicy bits of information about prominent people," said Locke, "and we're always glad to receive any information that is news."

"Nix on that hooey," said Mason. "You know what happened. And I know what happened. A list was made up, and Harrison Burke's name wasn't on that list. Neither was the name of the woman who was with him. Now, is it worth a thousand dollars to you to have absolute proof who that woman was?"

"No," said Locke, firmly and decisively.

"Well, that's all right," said Mason hastily. "Is it worth five hundred to you?"

"No."

"Well," insisted Mason, putting a whining note in his voice, "I tell you what I'll do. I'll let you have it for four hundred dollars. And that's absolutely bottom price. I've got another market that's offering three hundred and fifty. I've gone to a lot of trouble getting you located, and it's going to take four hundred for you to sit in."

"Four hundred is a lot of money."

"The information I've got," said Mason, "is a lot of information."

"You'd have to give me something besides the information," said Locke. "I'd want something we could use as proof if we ran into a libel suit."

"Sure," said Mason, "you give me the four hundred dollars when I give you the proof."

Locke was silent for a few seconds. Then he said, "Well, I'll have to think it over a little while. I'll call you back and let you know."

"I'll wait here at this number," Mason said. "You call me back here," and hung up.

He sat on a stool at the ice cream counter and drank a glass of plain carbonated water, without haste and without showing any emotion. His eyes were thoughtful, but his manner was calm.

At the end of six or seven minutes the telephone rang

again, and Mason answered it. "Smith talking," he whined.

Locke's voice came over the wire. "Yes, we'd be willing to pay that price provided we could get the proof."

"Okay," said Mason, "you be in your office tomorrow morning, and I'll get in touch with you there. But don't back out on me now, because I'm turning down this three hundred and fifty dollar offer."

"Listen, I'd like to see you tonight and get the thing cleaned up right now." There was a certain quaver of excitement in Locke's voice.

"You can't do that," Mason told him. "I could give you the information tonight, but I can't give you the proofs until tomorrow."

"Well," insisted Locke, "you could give me the information tonight, and then I'd pay you when you brought in the proofs tomorrow."

Mason gave a mocking laugh. "Now *I'll* tell one," he said.

Locke said, irritably: "Oh, well, have it your own way."

Mason chuckled. "Thanks," he said, "I think I will," and hung up the receiver.

He walked back to his automobile and sat in it for almost twenty minutes. At the end of that time, Frank Locke came out of the hotel, accompanied by a young woman. He had been shaved and massaged until his skin showed a trace of red under its sallow brown. He had the smugly complacent air of a man of the world, who rather enjoys knowing his way about.

The young woman with him was not over twenty-one or two, if one could judge by her face. She had a well curved figure, which was displayed to advantage; a perfectly expressionless face; expensive garments and just the faintest suggestion of too much make-up about her. She was beautiful in a certain full blown manner.

Perry Mason waited until they had taken a taxi, then

31

he went into the hotel, and walked over to the telephone desk.

The girl looked up with anxious eyes, put a surreptitious hand to the front of her waist, and pulled out a piece of paper.

On the piece of paper had been scribbled a telephone number: Freyburg 629803.

Perry Mason nodded to her and slipped the piece of paper in his pocket.

"Was that the conversation—that line about paying for information?" he asked.

"I can't divulge what went over the line."

"I know," said Mason, "but you'd tell me if that *wasn't* the conversation, wouldn't you?"

"Maybe," she said.

"All right, then, are you telling me anything?"

"No!"

"That's all I wanted to know," he told her, and grinned.

4

PERRY MASON WALKED INTO THE DETECTIVE BUREAU AT Police Headquarters.

"Drumm in here?" he asked.

One of the men nodded, and jerked a thumb toward an inner door.

Perry Mason walked in.

"Sidney Drumm," he said to one of the men who was sitting on the corner of a desk, smoking. Some one raised his voice, and yelled: "Oh, Drumm, come on out."

A door opened, and Sidney Drumm looked around until he saw Perry Mason, then grinned.

"Hello, Perry," he said.

He was a tall, thin man, with high cheek bones, and washed-out eyes. He would have looked more natural with a green eye-shade on his forehead, a pen behind his ear, keeping a set of books on a high stool, than in the Detective Bureau at Police Headquarters, which was, perhaps, why he made such a good detective.

Mason jerked his head and said, "I think I've got something, Sidney."

"Okay," said Drumm, "be right with you."

Mason nodded and walked out into the corridor. Sidney Drumm joined him in about five minutes.

"Shoot," he said.

"I'm chasing down a witness in something that may be of value to you," Mason said to the detective. "I don't know yet just where it's going to lead. Right now, I'm working for a client, and I want to get the low down on a telephone number."

"What telephone number?"

"Freyburg 629803," said Mason. "If it's the party I think it is, he'll be as wise as a treeful of owls, and we can't pull any of this wrong number business on him. I think it's probably an unlisted number. You've got to get it right from the records of the telephone company, and I have an idea you'd better do it personally."

Drumm said: "Gee, guy, you've got a crust!"

Perry Mason looked hurt.

"I told you I was working for a client," he said, "there's twenty-five bucks in it for you. I thought you'd be willing to take a run down to the telephone company for twenty-five bucks."

Drumm grinned.

"Why the hell didn't you say so in the first place?" he said. "Wait till I get my hat. We go down in your car or in mine?"

33

"Better take both," Mason said. "You go in yours, and I'll go in mine. I may not be coming back this way."

"Okay," the detective said. "I'll meet you down there."

Mason went out, got in his machine, and drove to the main office of the telephone company. Drumm, in a police car, was there ahead of him.

"I got to figuring," said Drumm, "that it might be better if you didn't go up there with me when I got the dope. So I've been up and got it for you."

"What is it?"

"George C. Belter," Drumm told him. "And the address is 556 Elmwood. You were right about its being an unlisted number. It's supposed to be airtight. Information can't even give out the number, let alone any information about it. So forget where you got it."

"Sure," agreed Mason, pulling two tens and a five from his pocket.

Drumm's fingers closed over the money.

"Baby," he said, "these look good after that poker game I was in last night. Come around again some time when you've got another client like this one."

"I may have this client for some time," Mason observed.

"That'll be fine," Drumm said.

Mason got in his car. His face was grim as he stepped on the starter and sent the machine speeding out toward Elmwood Drive.

Elmwood Drive was in the more exclusive residential district of the city. Houses, set well back from the street, were fronted with bits of lawn, and the grounds were ornamented with well-kept hedges and trees. Mason slid his car to a stop before five hundred and fifty-six. It was a pretentious house, occupying the top of a small knoll. There were no other houses within some two hundred feet on either side, and the knoll had been landscaped to set off the magnificence of the house.

Mason didn't drive his car into the driveway, but

parked it in the street, and went on foot to the front door. A light was burning on the porch. The evening was hot, and myriad insects clustered about the light, beating their wings against the big globe of frosted glass which surrounded the incandescent.

When he had rung the second time, the door was opened by a butler in livery. Perry Mason took one of his cards from his pocket, and handed it to the butler.

"Mr. Belter," he said, "wasn't expecting me, but he'll see me."

The butler glanced at the card, and stood to one side.

"Very good, sir. Will you come in, sir?"

Perry Mason walked into a reception room, and the butler indicated a chair. Mason could hear him climbing stairs. Then he heard voices from an upper floor, and the sound of the butler's feet coming down the stairs again.

The butler stepped into the room, and said: "I beg your pardon, but Mr. Belter doesn't seem to know you. Could you tell me what it was you wanted to see him about?"

Mason looked at the man's eyes, and said, shortly, "No."

The butler waited a moment, thinking that Mason might add to the comment, then, as nothing was said, turned and went back up the stairs. This time he was gone three or four minutes. When he returned, his face was wooden.

"Please step this way," he said. "Mr. Belter will see you."

Mason followed the man up the stairs and into a sitting room which was evidently one of a suite which opened from the hallway, taking up an entire wing of the house. The room was furnished with an eye to comfort and none for style. The chairs were massive and comfortable. No attempt had been made to follow any particular scheme of decoration, and the room radiated a masculinity which was untempered by feminine taste.

A door to an inner room swung open, and a big man stood on the threshold.

Perry Mason had a chance to look past this man, into the room from which he had emerged. It was a room fitted up as a study with book cases lining the walls, a massive desk and swivel chair in one corner, and, beyond that, a glimpse of a tiled bathroom.

The man stepped into the room and pulled the door closed behind him.

He was a huge bulk of a man with a face that was fat and pasty. There were puffs under his eyes. His chest was deep and his shoulders very broad. His hips were narrow, and Mason had the impression that the legs were probably thin. It was the eyes that commanded attention. They were hard as diamonds and utterly cold.

For a second or two the man stood near the door, staring at Mason. Then he walked forward, and his gait strengthened the impression that his legs were taxed to capacity to carry about the great weight of his torso.

Mason surmised that the man was somewhere in the late forties, and there was that in his manner which indicated he was completely cruel and ruthless in his dealings.

Standing, Mason was a good four inches shorter than this man, although his shoulders were as broad.

"Mr. Belter?" he asked.

The man nodded, planted his feet wide apart, and stared at Mason.

"What do you want?" he snapped.

Mason said, "I'm sorry to come to your house, but I wanted to talk over a matter of business."

"What about?"

"About a certain story that *Spicy Bits* threatens to publish. I don't want it published."

The diamond-hard eyes never so much as changed expression. They stared fixedly at Perry Mason.

"Why come here about it?" asked Belter.

"Because I think you're the one that I want to see."

"Well, I'm not."

36

"I think you are."

"I'm not. Don't know anything at all about *Spicy Bits*. I've read the sheet once in a while. It's a dirty, black-mailing rag, if you ask me."

Mason's eyes became hard. His body seemed to lean forward slightly from the hips.

"All right," he said. "I'm not asking you, I'm *telling* you."

"Telling me what?" Belter asked.

"Telling you that I'm an attorney, and I'm representing a client that *Spicy Bits* is trying to blackmail, and I don't like the set-up. I'm telling you that I don't intend to pay the price that's demanded, and I'm telling you further that I don't intend to pay a damned cent. I'm not going to buy any advertising in your sheet, and your sheet isn't going to publish the story about my client. Get that, and get it straight!"

Belter sneered. "It serves me right," he said, "for seeing the first shyster ambulance chaser that comes pounding at the door. I should have had the butler kick you out. You're either drunk or crazy. Or both. Personally, I have an idea it's both. Now are you going to get out, or shall I call the police?"

"I'll get out," Mason said, "when I finish what I was saying. You've kept in the background in this thing, and had Locke for your goat to stand out in front and take it. You've sat back and raked in the cash. You've received dividends out of blackmail. All right. Here's where you get an assessment."

Belter stood staring at Mason, saying nothing.

"I don't know whether you know who I am, or whether you know what I want," Mason went on, "but you can find out pretty quick by getting in touch with Locke. I'm telling you that if *Spicy Bits* publishes anything about my client, I'll rip off the mask of the man who owns the damned rag! Do you get that?"

"All right," Belter remarked. "You've made your threat.

Now I'll make mine. I don't know who you are, and I don't give a damn. Maybe *your* reputation is sufficiently spotless so that you can afford to go around and make threats. Then again, maybe it isn't. Perhaps you'd better watch some of your own fences before you start throwing mud over other people's."

Mason nodded curtly. "Of course, I expected that," he said.

"Well," Belter said, "you won't be disappointed then. But don't think that's an admission that I'm mixed up with *Spicy Bits*. I don't know a damned thing about it. And I don't want to. Now get out!"

Mason turned and walked through the door.

The butler was on the threshold. He spoke to Belter.

"I beg your pardon, sir, but your wife wants very much to see you before she goes out, and she's just leaving."

Belter walked toward the door. "All right," he said. "Take a good look at this man, Digley. If you ever see him on the place again, throw him off. Call a cop if you have to."

Mason turned and stared at the butler.

"Better call two cops, Digley," he observed. "You might need 'em."

He walked down the stairs, conscious of the fact that the other two men were descending immediately behind him. As he reached the lower hallway, a woman glided out from a corner near the door.

"I hope I didn't interrupt you, George," she said, "but . . ."

Her eyes met those of Perry Mason.

She was the woman who had called on Mason at his office, and given the name of Eva Griffin.

Her face drained of color. The blue eyes became dark with sudden panic. Then, by an effort, she controlled the expression of her face, and the blue eyes enlarged to that

38

wide-eyed stare of baby innocence which she had practiced when she had been in the office with Mason.

Mason's face showed nothing whatever. He stared at the woman with eyes that were perfectly calm and serene.

"Well?" asked Belter. "What's the matter?"

"Nothing," she said, and her voice sounded thin and frightened. "I just didn't know you were busy. I'm sorry I disturbed you."

Belter said, "Don't mind him. He's just a shyster who got in under false pretenses—and is leaving in a hurry."

Mason whirled on his heel.

"Listen, you," he said, "I'm going to tell you . . ."

The butler grabbed his arm. "This way, sir," he said.

Mason's powerful shoulders swung in a pivot that was like the swing of a golf professional. The butler was hurled across the hallway and slammed against the wall with a force that jarred the pictures on their hangings. Perry Mason strode directly to the massive form of George Belter.

"I decided to give you a break," he said, "and now I've changed my mind. You publish a word about my client, or about me in your sheet, and you'll go to jail for the next twenty years. D'you hear?"

The diamond-hard eyes stared at him with the uncordial glitter of a snake's eyes staring into the face of a man armed with a club. George Belter's right hand was in his coat pocket.

"It's a good thing," he said, "that you stopped right when you did. Make a move to lay a hand on me, and I'll blow your heart out! I've got witnesses to show it's self-defense, and I don't know but what it wouldn't be a good thing to do anyway."

"Don't bother," Mason said, evenly, "you can't stop me that way. There are others who know what I know, and know where I am and why."

Belter's lip curled.

"The trouble with you is," he said, "that you keep

singing the same tune. You've already played that game for all that it's worth. If you think that I'm afraid of anything that a cheap, blackmailing ambulance chaser can try to pin on me, you're mistaken. I'm telling you to get out, for the last time!"

Mason turned on his heel. "All right. I'm getting out. I've said all I've got to say."

George Belter's sarcastic comment reached his ears as he gained the door.

"At least twice," said Belter. "Some of it you've said three times."

5

EVA BELTER SAT IN PERRY MASON'S PRIVATE OFFICE, AND sobbed quietly into a handkerchief.

Perry Mason sat behind the desk with his coat off, and watched her with wary eyes and an entire absence of sympathy.

"You shouldn't have done it," she said, between sniffs.

"How was I supposed to know that?" asked Perry Mason.

"He's utterly ruthless," she said.

Mason nodded his head.

"I'm pretty ruthless myself," he observed.

"Why didn't you put the ad in the *Examiner?*"

"They wanted too much money. They seemed to think I was going to play Santy Claus."

"They knew it was important," she wailed. "There's a lot at stake."

Mason said nothing.

The woman sobbed silently for a moment, then raised her eyes, and stared in mute anguish at Perry Mason.

"You should never have threatened him," she said. "You should never have come to the house. You can't do anything with him by threats. Whenever he gets in a corner, he always fights his way out. He never asks for quarter, and he never gives any."

"Well, what's he going to do about it?" asked Mason.

"He'll ruin you," she sobbed. "He'll find every lawsuit that you've got, and accuse you of jury bribing, of suborning perjury, and of unprofessional conduct. He'll hound you out of the city."

"The minute he puts anything about me in his paper," said Mason, grimly, "I'll sue him for libel, and I'll keep on bringing a suit every time he mentions my name."

She shook her head with tears on her cheeks.

"You can't do that," she said, "He's too smart. He's got lawyers who tell him just what he can do, and just what he can't do. He'll get around behind your back, and frighten the judges who are sitting on your cases. He'll make the judges give adverse decisions. He'll keep under cover and fight you at every turn of the road."

Perry Mason drummed on the edge of his desk. "Baloney," he said.

"Oh, why," she wailed, "did you come out there? Why didn't you simply put an ad in the paper?"

Mason got to his feet.

"Now look here," he said. "I've heard enough of this. I went out there because I thought it was good business to go out there. That damned paper tried to hold me up, and I won't be held up by anybody. Your husband may be ruthless, but I'm pretty ruthless myself. *I've* never asked for quarter yet. And *I* won't give any."

He paused to stare down at her accusingly. "If you'd been frank with me when you came in here this thing wouldn't have happened. You had to go and lie about

41

the whole business, and that's the thing that's responsible for the present mess. It rests on your shoulders, not on mine."

"Don't be cross with me, Mr. Mason," she pleaded. "You're all I've got to depend on now. It's an awful mess, and you've got to see me through."

He sat down once more and said, "Don't lie to me then."

She looked down at her knees, adjusted the hem of her dress over her stocking, and plaited little folds in the garment with the tips of her gloved fingers.

"What shall we do?" she asked.

"One of the first things we'll do," he said, "is to begin at the beginning, and come clean."

"But you know all there is to know."

"All right then," said Mason, "tell me what I know, so that I can check up."

She frowned. "I don't understand."

"Go ahead," said Mason, "spill it. Tell me the whole business."

Her voice was thin and helpless. She continued to fold the cloth of the skirt over the top of her crossed legs. She did not look at him as she talked.

"Nobody," she said, "ever knew George Belter's connection with *Spicy Bits*. He kept it so much under cover that nobody ever suspected. Nobody at the office knew, except Frank Locke. And George could control Locke. He's got something terrible on him. I don't know just what it is. Maybe it's a murder.

"Anyway, none of our friends have ever suspected. They all think that George makes his money out of playing the stock market. I married George Belter seven months ago. I am his second wife. I guess I was fascinated by him and his money, but we've never got along well together. The last two months our relations have been strained. I was going to sue him for divorce. I think he knew it."

42

She paused to stare at Perry Mason, and saw no sympathy in his eyes.

"I was friendly with Harrison Burke," she went on. "I met him about two months ago. It was just a friendship. Nothing more. We were out together, and that murder took place. Of course, if Harrison Burke had to divulge my name, it would have ruined his career politically, because George would have sued me and named him as corespondent right away. I simply had to hush it up."

"Maybe your husband would never have found out," suggested Mason. "The District Attorney is a gentleman. Burke could have disclosed the facts to the District Attorney, and the District Attorney wouldn't have called you unless you had seen something that made your testimony absolutely necessary."

"You don't understand how they work," she told him. "I don't know all of it myself. But they've got spies everywhere. They buy pieces of information and run down odds and ends of gossip. Whenever a man gets prominent enough to attract attention, they go to a lot of trouble to get all the information they can about him. Harrison Burke is prominent politically, and he's coming up for re-election. They don't like him, and Burke knows it. I heard my husband telephoning to Frank Locke, and I knew that they were on the trail of the information. That was why I came to you. I wanted to buy them off before they had any idea of who it was that was with him."

"If your friendship with Burke was innocent," said Mason, "why don't you go to your husband and tell him what the situation is? After all, he'd be dragging his own name through the dust?"

She shook her head, vehemently.

"You don't know anything at all about it," she warned. "You simply don't understand my husband's character. You showed that in the way you handled him last night. He's savage and heartless. He's a fighter. What's more, he is money-mad. He knows that if I bring suit for divorce,

43

I will probably get some alimony and a lot of money for attorneys' fees, and suit money. All that he wants is to get something on me. If he could get something on me, and at the same time drag Harrison Burke's name through the courts, it would be a wonderful break for him."

Perry Mason frowned thoughtfully. "There's something funny about that high price they fixed," he remarked. "It seems to me that it's too high for political blackmail. Do you suppose that your husband or Frank Locke suspects who it is they're after?"

"No," she said firmly.

There was a moment of silence.

"Well," said Mason, "what do we do? Do we pay their price?"

"There won't be any price any more. George will call off all negotiations. He'll go ahead and fight. He figures that he can't afford to give in to you. If he does, he thinks that you'll hound him to death. That's the way he is, and that's the way he thinks everybody else is. He simply can't give in to anybody. It isn't in his nature, that's all."

Mason nodded, grimly. "All right, if he wants to fight, I'm perfectly willing to go to the mat with him. One of the first things I'll do will be to file suit against *Spicy Bits* the first time they mention my name, and I'll take the deposition of Frank Locke and force him to disclose who actually owns that paper. Or else I'll have him prosecuted for perjury. There are a lot of people who would like to see that sheet put where it belongs."

"Oh, you don't understand," she told him, speaking rapidly. "You don't understand the way they fight. You don't understand George. It would take a long while for you to get a libel suit to trial. He'll work fast. And then, you've got to remember that *I'm* your client. *I'm* the one you're supposed to protect. Long before any of that happens, *I'll* be ruined. They'll go after that Harrison Burke business hammer and tongs now."

Mason drummed on his desk again, and then said,

"Look here. You've hinted at some information your husband has that holds Frank Locke in line. Now I have an idea that you know what that information is. Suppose you give it to me, and I'll see if I can't crack a whip over Frank Locke."

Her face was white as she looked at him.

"Do you know what you're saying?" she said. "Do you know what you are doing? Do you know what you're getting into? They'll kill you! It wouldn't be the first time. They've got affiliations in the underworld with gangsters and gunmen."

Mason held her eyes with his.

"What," he insisted, "do you know about Frank Locke?"

She shuddered and dropped her eyes. After an interval, she said, in a tired tone: "Nothing."

Mason said, impatiently: "Every time you come here, you lie to me. You're one of those baby-faced little liars that always gets by by deceit. Just because you're beautiful, you've managed to get by with it. You've deceived every man that ever loved you, every man you ever loved. Now you're in trouble, and you're deceiving me."

She stared at him with blazing indignation, either natural or assumed.

"You've no right to talk to me that way!"

"The hell I haven't," said Mason, grimly.

They stared at each other for a second or two.

"It was something down South," she said, meekly.

"What was?"

"The trouble that Locke got into. I don't know what it was. I don't know where it was. I only know it was some trouble, and that it was down South somewhere. It was some trouble over a woman. That is, that's the way it started. I don't know how it finished. It may have been a murder. I don't know. I know it's something, and I know it's something that George holds over him all the time. That's the only way George ever deals with anybody.

45

He gets something on them and holds it over them, and makes them do just as he wants."

Mason stared at her, and said, "That's the way he handles you."

"That's the way he tries to."

"Was that the way he made you marry him?" asked Mason.

"I don't know," she said. "No."

He laughed grimly.

"Well," she said, "what difference does it make?"

"Maybe not any. Maybe a lot. I want some more money." She opened her purse.

"I haven't got much more," she said. "I can give you three hundred dollars."

Mason shook his head.

"You've got a checking account," he said. "I've got to have more money. I'm going to have some expenses in this thing. I'm fighting for myself now as well as for you."

"I can't give you a check. I don't have any checking account. He won't let me. That's another way that he keeps people under his control, through money. I have to get money from him in cash, or get it some other way."

"What other way?" asked Mason.

She said nothing. She drew out a roll of bills from the purse. "There's five hundred dollars here, and it's every cent I've got."

"All right," said Mason. "Keep twenty-five and give me the rest."

He pressed a button in the side of the desk. The door to the outer office framed the inquiring features of Della Street.

"Make another receipt," said Mason, "to this woman. Make it the same way you made the other one, with reference to a ledger page. This is for four hundred and seventy-five dollars, and it's on account."

Eva Belter passed the money over to Mason. He took it and gave it to Della Street.

46

The two women maintained toward each other that air of aloof hostility which characterizes two dogs walking stiff-legged, one around the other.

Della Street held her chin high, as she took the money, and returned to the outer office.

"She'll give you a receipt," said Perry Mason, "as you go out. How about getting in touch with you?"

She said, quickly enough: "That's all right. Ring the house. Ask for my maid and tell her that you're the cleaner. Tell her you can't find the dress I inquired about. I'll explain to her, and she'll pass the message on to me. Then I'll call you."

Mason laughed.

"You've got that down pat," he said. "You must have used it often."

She looked up at him, and her blue eyes set in a wide stare of tearful innocence.

"I'm sure," she said, "I don't know what you mean."

Mason pushed back his swivel chair, got to his feet, and walked around the desk.

"In the future," he told her, "you can save yourself the trouble of putting on that baby stare with me if you want to. I think we understand each other pretty well. You're in a jam and I'm trying to get you out."

She got to her feet slowly, looked into his eyes, and suddenly put her hands on his shoulders.

"Somehow," she said, "you inspire me with confidence. You're the only man I ever knew who could stand up to my husband. I feel as though I could cling to you and you'd protect me."

She tilted back her face so that her lips were close to his, and her eyes were staring into his. Her body was quite close to his.

He took her elbow in his long, strong fingers and turned her away from him.

"I'll protect you," he said, "just as long as you pay cash."

47

She squirmed around so that she was facing him again

"Don't you ever think of anything except money?" she asked.

"Not in this game."

"You're all I've got to depend on," she wailed. "Everything in the world. You're all that stands between me and utter ruin."

"That," he said coolly, "is my business. It's what I'm here for."

As he talked, he had been walking with her toward the door of the outer office. As he put his right hand on the knob, she twisted around so that she was free of his grip.

"Very well," she said, "and thank you."

Her tone was formal, almost frigid. She walked through the office door and into the outer office.

Perry Mason closed the door behind her. He went to his desk, picked up the telephone and when he heard Della Street's voice, said, "Give me an outside line, Della."

He gave the number of Drake's Detective Bureau, asked for Paul Drake, and got him on the line.

"Listen, Paul," he said, "this is Perry. I've got a job for you. You've got to handle it quickly. Frank Locke, down at *Spicy Bits,* is a devil with the women. He's got a jane over at the Wheelright Hotel that he's running around with. She lives there. He drops into the barber shop once in a while and gets himself all prettied up before he takes her out on a date. He came from the South some place. I don't know just where. And he was mixed up in something when he left there. Frank Locke probably isn't his real name. I want you to put enough men on him to find out what it's all about, and do it quick. How much is it going to set me back?"

"Two hundred dollars," said Paul Drake's voice. "And another two hundred dollars at the end of the week, if I work on it that long."

"I don't think I can pass this on to my client," said Mason.

"Make it three twenty-five in all, then and use me right you find you can put it in on the expense account ter."

"Okay," said Mason. "Get started."

"Wait a minute. I was just going to call you anyway. see a big Lincoln is parked down here in front of the uilding, with a chauffeur sitting at the wheel. I have a unch that it's the same car that your mysterious lady riend used for a get-away the other day. Do you want ne to chase it down? I took the license number as I :ame up."

"No," said Mason. "That's okay. I've got her tagged. Forget about her and start in on this Locke business."

"All right," said Drake, and hung up.

Perry Mason dropped the receiver into place.

Della Street stood in the doorway.

"She gone?" asked Mason.

Della Street nodded.

"That woman's going to make you trouble," she said.

"You told me that before," said Mason.

"All right, I'm telling it to you again."

"Why?" said Mason.

"I don't like the way she looks," said Della Street. "And I don't like the way she acts toward a working girl. She's got that snobby complex."

"Lots of people are like that, Della."

"I know, but she's different. She doesn't know what honesty means. She loves trickery. She'd turn on you in a second if it would be to her advantage."

Perry Mason's face was thoughtful.

"It wouldn't be to her advantage," he remarked, his voice preoccupied.

Della Street stared at him for a moment, then softly closed the door and left him alone.

6

HARRISON BURKE WAS A TALL MAN WHO CULTIVATED AN
air of distinction. His record in Congress had been
mediocre, but he had identified himself as "The Friend of
the People" by sponsoring legislation which a clique of
politicians pushed through the House, knowing that it
would never pass the upper body, or, if it did, that it
would be promptly vetoed by the President.

He was planning his campaign for the Senate by
adroitly seeking to interest the more substantial class of
citizens and impress them with the fact that he was, at
heart, conservative. He was trying to do this without in
any way sacrificing his following among the common
people, or his reputation as being a friend of the people.

He looked at Perry Mason, his eyes shrewd, and ap
praising, and remarked: "But I don't understand what
you're driving at."

"All right," Mason said, "if I've got to hand it to you
straight from the shoulder, I'm talking about the night of
the Beechwood stick-up, and your presence in the Inn
with a married woman."

Harrison Burke winced as though he had been struck a
blow. He took a deep breath that was a gasp, then delib
erately set his face in lines that he doubtless thought
were wooden.

"I think," he said in his deep, booming voice, "that
you have been misinformed. And inasmuch as I am

50

exceedingly busy this afternoon, I will have to ask you to excuse me."

Perry Mason's expression was a mixture of disgust and resentment. Then he took a step toward the politician's desk and stared down at the man's face.

"You're in a jam," he said, slowly, "and the quicker you get done pulling that line of hooey, the quicker we can talk about getting out of it."

"But," protested Burke, "I don't know anything about you. You haven't any credentials, or anything."

"This is a case," Mason answered, "where you don't need any credentials except knowledge. I've got the knowledge. I'm representing the woman who was with you on that occasion. *Spicy Bits* is going to publish the whole thing and demand that you be taken before the Coroner's Jury and the Grand Jury and made to tell what you know, and who was with you."

Harrison Burke's face turned a sickly gray. He leaned forward on his desk as though he wanted support for his arms and shoulders.

"What?" he asked.

"You heard what I said."

"But," said Burke, "I never knew. She never told me. That is, this is the first I knew about it. I'm sure there must be some mistake."

"All right," said Mason. "Guess again. There isn't any mistake."

"How does it happen that I hear of this through you?"

"Because," said Mason, "the lady probably doesn't want to go near you. She's got herself to think about, and she's trying to work her way out of it. I'm doing the best I can, and it takes money. She's probably not the kind that would call on you for a campaign contribution. I am."

"You want money?" asked Burke.

"What the hell did you think I wanted?"

Harrison Burke seemed to be getting the full signif-

51

icance of his predicament in a series of waves which penetrated his consciousness, one at a time.

"My God!" he said. "It would ruin me!"

Perry Mason said nothing.

"*Spicy Bits* can be bought off," continued the politician. "I don't know just how they work it. It's some kind of a deal by which you buy advertising space and then don't live up to the contract. They have a clause in there for liquidated damages, I understand. You're a lawyer. You should know about that. And you should know how to handle it."

"*Spicy Bits* can't be bought off now," said Mason. "In the first place they wanted too much money. And in the second place, they're out for blood now. It's a question of no quarter given, and no quarter asked."

Harrison Burke drew himself up. "My dear man," he said, "I think you are entirely mistaken. I see no reason why the paper should adopt that attitude."

Mason grinned at him, "You don't?"

"Certainly not," said Burke.

"Well, it happens that the power behind the throne in that paper, the man who really owns it, is George C. Belter. And the woman you were out with is his wife, who was contemplating suing him for divorce. Think that over."

Burke's face was the color of putty.

"That's impossible," he said. "Belter wouldn't be mixed up in anything like that. He's a gentleman."

"He may be a gentleman, but he owns the sheet," said Mason.

"Oh, but he couldn't!" protested Burke.

"Well, he does," Mason repeated. "I'm giving you the information. Take it or leave it. It's not my funeral. It's yours. If you get out of this, it'll be because you play your cards right and have some good advice. I'm ready to give you the advice."

Harrison Burke twisted his fingers together. "Exactly what is it that you want?" he asked.

Mason said, "There's only one way I know of to break that gang, and that's to fight it with fire. They're blackmailers, and I'm going to do some blackmailing myself. I've got some information that I'm trying to chase down. It's costing money. The woman is out of money, and I don't intend to finance it myself.

"Every time the hour hand on that clock makes a circle, it means that I've put in more of my time, and that other people have put in more of their time. Expenses keep running up. As I see it, there's no reason why you shouldn't be called on to do your share."

Harrison Burke blinked. "How much do you think it will cost?" he inquired, cautiously.

"I want fifteen hundred dollars now, and if I get you out of it, it's going to cost you more."

Burke wet his lips with the tip of his tongue. "I'll have to think it over," he said. "If I'm going to raise any money, I'll have to make some arrangements to get it. You come back tomorrow morning, and I'll let you know."

"This thing is moving fast," Mason told him. "There'll be a lot of water gone under the bridge between now and tomorrow morning."

"Come back in two hours, then," said Burke.

Mason looked at the man and said, "All right. Listen, here's what you're planning to do. You're going to look me up. I'll tell you in advance what you'll find. You'll find that I'm a lawyer that has specialized in trial work, and in a lot of criminal work. Every fellow in this practice cultivates some sort of a specialty. I'm a specialist on getting people out of trouble. They come to me when they're in all sorts of trouble, and I work them out. Most of my cases never come to court.

"If you look me up through some family lawyer or some corporation lawyer, he'll probably tell you that I'm a shyster. If you look me up through some chap in the

District Attorney's office, he'll tell you that I'm a dangerous antagonist but he doesn't know very much about me. If you look me up through a bank you won't find out a damned thing."

Burke opened his mouth to speak, then thought better of it and was silent.

"Now maybe that information will cut down the amount of time you're going to take to look me up," went on Mason. "If you call up Eva Belter, she'll probably be sore because I came to you. She wants to handle it all by herself. Or else she's never thought of you. I don't know which. If you call her up, ask for her maid and leave some message with the maid about a dress or something. Then she'll call you back."

Harrison Burke looked surprised.

"How did you know that?" he asked.

"That's the way she gets her messages," said Mason. "Mine's to tell about a dress. What's yours?"

"About the delivery of shoes," Harrison Burke blurted.

"It's a good system," Mason said, "providing she doesn't get her wearing apparel mixed. And I'm not so sure about her maid."

Burke's reserve seemed to have melted.

"The maid," he said, "doesn't know anything. She simply delivers the message. Eva keeps the code. I didn't know that she had any one else who used that sort of a code."

Perry Mason laughed.

"Be your age," he said.

"As a matter of fact," said Harrison Burke, with dignity, "Mrs. Belter called me on the telephone not over an hour ago. She said that she was in serious difficulties and had to raise a thousand dollars at once. She wanted me to help her. She didn't say what the money was for."

Mason whistled.

"Well," he said, "that makes it different. I was afraid she wasn't going to make you kick in. I don't care how you come through, but I think you should help carry the load. I'm working for you just as much as I am for her, and it's a fight that's running into money."

Burke nodded. "Come back in half an hour," he said, "and I'll let you know."

Mason moved toward the door. "All right," he remarked, "make it half an hour then. And you'd better get the money in cash. Because you won't want to have any checks going through your bank account, in case there should be any publicity about what I'm doing or whom I'm representing."

Burke pushed back his chair, and made a politician's tentative motion of extending his hand. Perry Mason did not see the hand, or, if he did, he did not bother to acknowledge it, but strode toward the door.

"Half an hour," he said, on the threshold, and slammed the door behind him.

As he put his hand on the door catch of his automobile, a man tapped him on the shoulder.

Mason turned.

The man was a heavy-set individual with impudent eyes.

"I want an interview, Mr. Mason," he said.

"Interview?" said Mason. "Who the hell are you?"

"I'm Crandall," said the man. "A reporter for *Spicy Bits*. We're interested in the doings of prominent people, Mr. Mason. And I'd like an interview with you as to what you discussed with Harrison Burke."

Slowly, deliberately, Perry Mason took his hand from the automobile door catch, turned around on his heel, and surveyed the man.

"So," he said, "that's the kind of tactics you folks are going to use, is it?"

Crandall continued to stare with his impudent eyes.

"Don't get hard," he said, "because it won't buy you anything."

"The hell it won't," said Perry Mason. He measured

55

the distance, and slammed a straight left full into the grinning mouth.

Crandall's head shot back. He staggered for two steps, then went down like a sack of meal.

Passing pedestrians paused to stare, and collected in a little group.

Mason paid no attention to them, but turned, jerked open the door of his machine, got in, slammed the door shut, stepped on the starter, and pushed the car out into traffic.

From a nearby drug store, he called Harrison Burke's office.

When he had Burke on the line, he said, "Mason talking, Burke. Better not go out. And better get somebody to act as a bodyguard. The paper we talked about has got a couple of strong arm men sticking around, ready to muscle into your business in any way that'll do the most damage. When you get that money for me, send it over to my office by messenger. Get somebody you can trust and don't tell them what's in the package. Put it in a sealed envelope, as though it might be papers."

Harrison Burke started to say something.

Perry Mason savagely slammed the receiver on the hook, strode out of the telephone booth and into his car.

7

A STORM WAS WHIPPING UP FROM THE SOUTHEAST. SLOW, leaden clouds drifted across the night sky, and bombarded the ground with great mushrooms of spattering water.

Wind was tugging at the corners of the apartment house where Perry Mason lived. A window was open only about half an inch at the bottom, but enough wind came through that opening to billow the curtains and keep them flapping.

Mason sat up in bed and groped for the telephone in the dark. He found the instrument, put it to his ear and said, "Hello."

The voice of Eva Belter sounded swift and panic-stricken over the wire.

"Thank God I've got you! Get in your car and come at once! This is Eva Belter."

Perry Mason was still sleepy.

"Come where?" he said. "What's the matter?"

"Something awful has happened," she said. "Don't come to the house. I'm not there."

"Where are you?"

"I'm down at a drug store on Griswold Avenue. Drive out the Avenue and you'll see the lights in the drug store. I'll be standing in front of it."

Perry Mason was getting his faculties together.

"Listen," he said, "I've answered night calls before, where people have been trying to take me for a ride. Let's make sure that there isn't anything phony about this."

She screamed at him over the telephone.

"Oh, don't be so damned cautious! Come out here at once. I tell you I'm in serious trouble. You can recognize my voice all right."

Mason said calmly, "Yes. I know all that. What was the name you gave me the first time you came to the office?"

"Griffin!" she shrieked.

"Okay," said Mason. "Coming out."

He climbed into his clothes, slipped a revolver in his hip pocket, pulled on a raincoat, and a cap which came down low over his forehead, switched out the lights, and left the apartment. His car was in the garage, and he nursed it into action, moved out into the rain before the motor was fully warmed.

The car spat and back-fired as he turned the corner. Mason kept the choke out and stepped on the gas. Rain whipped against the windshield. Little geysers of water mushroomed up from the pavement where the big drops splashed down were turned to brilliance by the illumination of his headlights.

Mason ignored the possibility of any other traffic on the road as he swept past the intersections with increasing speed. He turned to the right on Griswold Avenue, and ran for a mile and a half before he slowed down and commenced to look for lights.

He saw her standing in front of a drug store. She had on a coat and no hat, and was heedless of the rain, which had soaked her hair thoroughly. Her eyes were wide and scared.

Perry Mason swung into the curb and brought the car to a stop.

"I thought you'd never get here," she said, as he opened the door for her.

She climbed in, and Perry saw that she wore an evening gown, satin shoes, and a man's coat. She was soaking wet and water trickled down to the floorboards of the car.

"What's the trouble?" Perry Mason asked.

She stared at him with her white, wet face, and said, "Drive out to the house, quick!"

"What's the trouble?" he repeated.

"My husband's been murdered," she wailed.

Mason snapped on the dome light in the car.

"Don't do that!" she said.

He looked at her face. "Tell me about it," he said, calmly.

"Will you get this car started?"

"Not until I know the facts," he replied, almost casually.

"We've got to get there before the police do."

"Why have we?"

"Because we've *got* to."

Mason shook his head. "No," he said, "we're not going to talk to the police until I know exactly what happened."

"Oh," she said, "it was terrible!"

"Who killed him?"

"I don't know."

"Well, what *do* you know?"

"Will you turn off that damned light?" she snapped.

"After you've finished telling me what happened," he persisted.

"What do you want it on for?"

"The better to see you with, my dear," he said, but there was no humor in his voice. His manner was grim.

She sighed wearily. "I don't know what happened. I think it was somebody that he'd been blackmailing. I could hear their voices from the upper floor. They were very angry. I went to the stairs to listen."

"Could you hear what was being said?"

"No," she said, "just words and the tone. I could hear that they were cursing. Every once in a while there would be a word. My husband was using that cold, sarcastic tone that he gets when he's fighting mad. The other man had his voice raised, but he wasn't shouting. He was interrupting my husband every once in a while."

"Then what happened?"

"Then I crept up the stairs because I wanted to hear what was being said." She paused, catching her breath.

"All right," pressed Mason, "go on. What happened then?"

"And then," she said, "I heard the shot and the sound of a falling body."

"Just the one shot?"

"Just the one shot, and the sound of the body falling. Oh, it was terrible! It jarred the house."

"All right," said Mason. "Go on from there. Then what did you do?"

"Then," she said, "I turned and ran. I was afraid."

"Where did you run?"

"To my room."

"Did anybody see you?"

"No, I don't think so."

"Then what did you do?"

"I waited there a minute."

"Did you hear anything?"

"Yes, I heard the man who had fired the shot run down the stairs and out of the house."

"All right," Mason said insistently, "then what happened?"

"Then," she said, "I decided that I must go and see George and see what could be done for him. I went up to his study. He was in there. He'd been taking a bath, and had thrown a bathrobe around himself. He was lying there—dead."

"Lying where?" pressed Mason, remorselessly.

"Oh, don't make me be so specific," she snapped. "I can't tell you. It was some place near the bathroom. He'd just come out of his bath. He must have been standing in the bathroom door when this argument took place."

"How do you know he was dead?"

"I could tell by looking at him. That is, I think he was dead. Oh, I'm not sure. Please come out and help me. If he isn't dead, it's all right. There won't be any trouble. If he is, we're all of us in a hell of a mess."

"Why?"

"Because everything's going to come out. Don't you see? Frank Locke knows all about Harrison Burke, and he'll naturally think that Harrison Burke killed him. That will make Burke mention my name, and then anything may happen. Suspicion may even shift to me."

Mason said, "Oh, forget it. Locke knows about Burke all right. But Locke is nothing but a lightweight and a figurehead. As soon as he loses your husband as a prop, he won't be able to stand up. Don't think for a minute

60

that Harrison Burke was the only man who had it in for your husband."

"No," she insisted, "but Harrison Burke had the motive, more so than any of the others. The others didn't know who ran the paper. Harrison Burke knew. You told him."

"So he told you *that*, eh?" said Mason.

"Yes, he told me that. What did you have to go to him for?"

"Because," said Mason, grimly, "I wasn't going to take him for a free ride. He was getting a lot of service, and I intended to make him pay for it. I wasn't going to have you put up all the money."

"Don't you think," she said, "that that was something for me to decide?"

"No."

She bit her lip, started to say something, then changed her mind.

"All right," he said. "Now listen and get this straight. If he's dead there's going to be a lot of investigation. You've got to keep your nerve. Have you any idea who it was that was in that house?"

"No," she said, "not to be sure, just what I could gather from the tone of the man's voice."

"All right," he told her. "That's something. You said you couldn't hear what was being said?"

"I couldn't," she said, slowly, "but I could hear the sound of their voices. I could recognize the tones. I heard my husband's voice, and then this other man's voice."

"Had you ever heard that other voice before?"

"Yes."

"Do you know who it was?"

"Yes."

"Well, don't be so damned mysterious," he said. "Who was it? I'm your lawyer. You've got to tell me."

She turned and faced him. "You know who it was," she said.

"*I* know?"

"Yes."

"Look here, one of us is crazy. How would I know who it was?"

"Because," she said, slowly, "it was you!"

His eyes became cold, hard and steady.

"Me?"

"Yes, you! Oh, I didn't want to tell! I wasn't going to let you think I knew. I was going to protect your secret! But you wormed it out of me. But I won't tell any one else, never, never, never! It's just a secret that you and I share."

He stared at her with his lips tightening. "So that's the kind of a playmate you are, eh?"

She met his eyes and nodded, slowly.

"Yes, Mr. Mason, I'm the sort you can trust. I'm never going to betray you."

He sucked in a deep breath, then sighed.

"Oh, hell," he said, "what's the use!"

There was a moment of silence. Then Perry Mason asked, in a voice that was entirely without expression: "Did you hear a car drive away—afterwards?"

She hesitated a moment, and then said: "Yes, I think I did, but the storm was making a lot of racket up there with the trees rubbing against the house and everything. But I think I heard a motor."

"Now listen," he told her. "You're nervous and you're unstrung. But if you're going to face a bunch of detectives and start talking that way, you're just going to get yourself into trouble. You'd either better have a complete breakdown and get a physician who will refuse to let any one talk with you, or else you'd better get your story licked into shape. Now you either heard a motor or you didn't hear one. Did you, or didn't you?"

"Yes," she said, defiantly, "I heard one."

"Okay," he said. "That's better. Now, how many people are in the house?"

"What do you mean?"

"Servants and everybody," he said. "Just who's there. I want to know everybody that's in that house."

"Well," she said, "there's Digley, the butler."

"Yes," said Mason, "I met him. I know all about him. Who else? Who is the housekeeper?"

"A Mrs. Veitch," she said, "and she has her daughter staying with her now. The daughter is there for a few days."

"All right, how about the men? Let's check up on the men. Just Digley, the butler?"

"No," she said, "there's Carl Griffin."

"Griffin, eh?"

She flushed. "Yes."

"That accounts for the fact that you used the name 'Griffin' when you came to call on me the first time?"

"No, it doesn't. I just used the first name that came into my mind. Don't say anything like that."

He grinned. "I didn't say anything like that. You're the one that said it."

She rushed into rapid conversation.

"Carl Griffin is my husband's nephew. He's very seldom home at night. He's pretty wild I guess. He leads a pretty gay life. They say he comes in drunk a good deal of the time. I don't know about that. But I know that he's very close to my husband. George comes as near having affection for Carl as he does for any living mortal. You must know that my husband is a queer man. He doesn't really love any one. He wants to own and possess, to dominate and crush, but he can't love. He hasn't any close friends and he's completely self-sufficient."

"Yes," said Mason, "I know all that stuff. It isn't your husband's character that I'm interested in. Tell me some more about this Carl Griffin. Was he there tonight?"

"No," she said, "he went out early in the evening. In fact, I don't think he was there for dinner. It seems to me that he went out to the golf club and played golf this afternoon. When did it start to rain?"

"Around six o'clock, I think," said Mason. "Why?"

"Yes," she said, "that's the way I remember it. It was pleasant this afternoon, and Carl was playing golf. Then I think George said that he had telephoned he was going to stay out at the golf club for dinner and wouldn't be in until late."

"You're *sure* he hadn't come in?" asked Mason.

"Certain."

"You're sure that it wasn't *his* voice that you heard up there in the room?"

She hesitated for a moment.

"No," she said, "it was yours."

Mason muttered an exclamation of annoyance.

"That is," she said hastily, "it sounded like yours. It was a man who talked just like you. He had that same quiet way of dominating a conversation. He could raise his voice, and yet make it seem quiet and controlled, just like you, but I'll never mention that to any one, never in the world! They could torture me, but I wouldn't mention your name."

She widened her blue eyes by an effort, and stared full into his face with that look of studied innocence.

Perry Mason stared at her, then shrugged his shoulders. "All right," he said, "we'll talk about that later. In the meantime you've got to get yourself together. Now were your husband and this other man quarreling about you?"

"Oh, I don't know. I don't know!" she said. "Can't you understand that I don't know what they were talking about? I only know that I *must* go back there. What will happen if somebody else should discover the body and I should be gone?"

Mason said, "That's all right, but you've waited this long, and a minute or two isn't going to make any great difference now. There's one thing I want to know before we go."

"What is it?"

He reached over and took her face and turned it until

64

the light from the globe in the top of the car was shining full on her face. Then he said, slowly, "Was it Harrison Burke that was up in the room with him when that shot was fired?"

She gasped. "My God, no!"

"Was Harrison Burke out there tonight?"

"No."

"Did he call you up tonight or this afternoon?"

"No," she said, "I don't know anything about Harrison Burke. I haven't seen him or heard from him since that night at the Beechwood Inn, and I don't want to. He has done nothing but bring trouble into my life."

Mason said, grimly: "Then, how did it happen that you knew that I had told him of your husband's connection with *Spicy Bits?*"

She dropped her eyes from his, tried to shake her head free of his hands.

"Go on," he said, remorselessly, "answer the question. Did he tell you that when he was out there tonight?"

"No," she muttered in a subdued voice. "He told me that when he telephoned me this afternoon."

"Then he did call up this afternoon, eh?"

"Yes."

"How soon after I had been at his office, do you know?"

"I think it was right after."

"Before he had sent me some money by messenger?"

"Yes."

"Why didn't you tell me that before? Why did you say that you hadn't heard from him?"

"I forgot," she said. "I did tell you earlier that he'd called up. If I had wanted to lie to you, I wouldn't have told you at first that I'd heard from him."

"Oh, yes, you would," said Mason. "You told me then because you didn't think there was any possibility that I would suspect him of having been in that room with your husband when the shot was fired."

"That's not so," she said.

65

He nodded his head slowly.

"You're just a little liar," he said, judicially and dispassionately. "You can't tell the truth. You don't play fair with anybody, not even yourself. You're lying to me right now. You know who that man was that was in the room."

She shook her head. "No, no, no, no," she said. "Won't you understand, I don't *know* who it was? I think it was you! That was why I didn't call you from the house. I ran down to this drug store to call you. It's almost a mile."

"Why did you do that?"

"Because," she said, "I wanted to give you time to get home. Don't you see? I wanted to be able to say that I called you and found you at your apartment, if I should be asked. It would have been awful to have called and found that you were out, after I recognized your voice."

"You didn't recognize my voice," he said quietly.

"I *thought* I did," she said demurely.

Mason said, "There's no thinking about it. I've been in bed for the last two or three hours, but I couldn't prove any alibi. If the police thought I'd been to the house I'd have the devil of a time trying to square myself. You've figured that all out."

She looked up at him and suddenly flung her arms around his neck.

"Oh, Perry," she said, "please don't look at me that way. Of course, I'm not going to tell on you. You're in this thing just as deep as I am. You did what you did to save me. We're in it together. I'm going to stand by you, and you're going to stand by me."

He pushed her away and put his fingers on her wet arm, until she had released her hold. Then he turned her face once more until he could look in her eyes.

"*We're* not in this thing a damned bit," he said. "You're my client, and I'm sticking by you. That's all. You understand that?"

"Yes," she said.

66

"Whose coat is that you're wearing?"

"Carl's. I found it in the corridor. I started out first in the rain, and then realized I would get soaking wet. There was a coat in the hallway, and I put it on."

"Okay. You be thinking that over while I'm driving up to the place. I don't know whether the police will be there or not. Do you know if any one else heard the shot?"

"No, I don't think they did."

"All right," he said, "if we've got an opportunity to go over this thing before the police get there, you forget this business about running down to the drug store and putting in the telephone call. Tell them that you called me from the house, and *then* you ran down the hill to meet me. And that was why you were wet. You couldn't stay in the house. You were afraid. Do you understand that?"

"Yes," she said, meekly.

Perry Mason switched out the dome light in the car and snapped back the gear lever, eased in the clutch, and started the machine boring through the rain.

She came over and cuddled closely to him, her left arm around his neck, her right arm resting on his leg.

"Oh," she wailed, "I'm so afraid, and I feel so alone."

"Shut up," he said, "and think!"

He drove the car at a savage pace up the long grade, turned on Elmwood Drive, and went into second as he climbed the knoll on which the big house was situated. He turned in at the driveway and parked the car directly in front of the porch.

"Now listen," he said to her in a low voice, as he helped her out, "the house seems to be quiet. Nobody else heard the shot. The police aren't here yet. You've got to use your head. If you've been lying to me, it will mean that you're going to get into serious difficulties."

"I haven't been lying," she said. "I told you the truth—honest to God."

"Okay," he said, and they sprinted across the porch.

"The door's unlocked. I left it unlocked," she said, "you

67

can go right in." And she hung back, in order to let him be the first to enter the house.

Perry Mason tried the door.

"No," he said, "it's locked. The night latch is on. Have you got your key?"

She looked at him blankly.

"No," she said, "my key's in my purse."

"Where's your purse?" he asked her.

She stared at him with eyes that were indistinct, but her pose was that of one who is rigid with terror.

"My God!" she said, "I must have left my purse up in the room with . . . . with my husband's body!"

"You had it with you when you went upstairs?" he asked.

"Yes," she said, "I know I did. But I must have dropped it. I don't remember having it with me when I came out."

"We've got to get in," he said. "Is there another door that's open?"

She shook her head, then suddenly said, "Yes, there's a back door where the servants come in. There's a key that we keep hanging up under the eaves of the garage. It will open the door, and we can get in that way."

"Let's go."

They walked down the steps from the porch and around the gravel driveway which circled the house. The house was dark and silent. Wind was lashing the shrubbery, and rain was pelting against the sides of the house, but no noise whatever came from the interior of the gloomy mansion.

"Don't make any noise," he cautioned her. "I want to get in without the servants hearing us. If nobody's awake, I want to have a minute or two to check things over after I see how the land lies inside."

She nodded, groped in the eaves of the garage, found the key, and opened the back door.

"All right," he said. "You sneak through the house and

let me in the front door. I'll lock this back door from the outside, and put the key back in the place on the nail."

She nodded her head and vanished in the darkness of the house. He closed the door, locked it, and put the key back where it had been; then he retraced his steps around the front of the house.

8

PERRY MASON REACHED THE FRONT DOOR AND STOOD there, waiting on the porch for what seemed to him to be two or three minutes before he heard Eva Belter's step and the click of the lock. She opened the door and smiled at him.

There was a light burning in the entrance hall, a night light which illuminated things vaguely, showing the dark stretch of stairs which led up to the upper floor, the furniture of the reception hallway, a couple of straight back chairs, an ornamental mirror, a coat rack, and umbrella stand.

There was a woman's coat on the rack, two canes, and three umbrellas in the stand. A trickle of rain water had oozed from the bottom of the stand where the umbrellas were kept, and made a puddle which reflected the rays of the night light.

"Look here," said Mason in a whisper. "You didn't turn out the light when you went out?"

"No," she said, "it was just like this when I left."

"You mean that your husband let some one come in

this door to see him without turning on any lights except that night light?"

"Yes," she said, "I guess so."

"Don't you ordinarily keep a brighter light burning over the stairs until the family has retired?"

"Sometimes," she said, "but George has his upstairs apartment all to himself. He doesn't bother the rest of us, and we don't bother him."

"All right," said Mason. "Let's go on up. Turn on the light."

She clicked a switch, and the stairway was flooded with light.

Mason led the way up the stairs and into the reception room of the suite where he had first seen George Belter.

The door through which Belter had entered on that occasion was now closed. Mason turned the knob, opened the door and stepped into the study.

It was a huge room, done in much the same style as the sitting room. The chairs were huge and heavily upholstered. The desk was twice the size of an ordinary large desk. There was a door open which led into a bedroom, and, within a few feet of that door, was the door which led into the bath. There was also a door from the bedroom to the bathroom.

The body of George Belter lay on the floor, just inside the doorway from the bathroom to the study. It was wrapped in a flannel dressing gown, which had fallen open along the front and showed that underneath the gown the body was entirely nude.

Eva Belter gave a little scream and clung closely to Mason. Mason shook her off, strode to the body, and knelt down.

The man was quite dead. There had been but one bullet, and that had penetrated directly through the heart. Death had apparently been instantaneous.

Mason felt the inside of the bathrobe and noticed that it was damp. He pulled the bathrobe together over the

70

corpse, stepped over the outstretched arm, and into the bathroom.

Like the other rooms of the suite, the bathroom was built on a massive scale, for a huge man. The bathtub, set down below the level of the floor, was some three or four feet deep and almost eight feet long. A huge washbowl occupied the center of the bathroom. There were towels folded on the racks. Mason looked at them, then turned to Eva Belter.

"Listen," he said, "he was taking a bath, and something caused him to get up and get out. Notice that he flung on his bathrobe, and didn't dry himself with a towel. He was still wet when he put the bathrobe around him, and the towels are all folded, and haven't been used."

She nodded slow acquiescence. "Do you suppose we had better moisten a bath towel and crumple it as though he had dried himself?" she asked.

"Why?"

"Oh, I don't know," she said. "I just wondered."

"Listen," he told her, "we get to faking evidence here, and we're going to get into serious difficulty. Now listen, and get this straight! Apparently, no one besides yourself knows what happened, or when. The police will get sore if they aren't notified right away. They'll also want to know how you happened to telephone to a lawyer before you telephoned them. It makes it look like a suspicious circumstance as far as you're concerned. D'you understand?"

She nodded again, her eyes wide and dark.

"All right," he said, "now get this, and get it straight, and keep your head all the way through. Here's what happened. You're going to tell exactly the truth, just as you told it to me, with one exception. And that is about your coming back upstairs after the man had left the house. That's the thing that I don't like about your story, and that's the thing that the police won't like about it. If you had presence of mind enough to go up the stairs and

71

look around, then you would have had presence of mind enough to call the police. The fact that you wanted to call an attorney before you called the police, is going to make the police think that you had a consciousness of guilt."

"But," she said, "we can explain to them that I had consulted you on this other matter, and that it was all so mixed up together that I wanted to talk with you before I talked with the police, couldn't we?"

He laughed at her.

"What a sweet mess *that* would be. Then the police would want to know all about what that other matter was. And before you got done, you'd find that you had given them the best kind of motive for you to kill your husband. That other matter can never come into the thing at all. We've got to get hold of Harrison Burke and see that he keeps his mouth closed."

"But," she protested, "how about the paper? How about *Spicy Bits?*"

"Has it ever occurred to you," he asked, "that, with your husband's death, you are the owner of that paper? You can step into the saddle, and control the policy right now."

"Suppose he left a will disinheriting me?"

"In that event," he said, "we'll file a suit contesting the will, and try and get you put in as a special administratrix, pending the determination of the suit."

"All right," she said, swiftly, "I ran out of the house, and then what happened?"

"Exactly the way you told it to me. You were so panic-stricken that you ran out of the house. And remember that you ran out *before* the man who was in the room with your husband ran down the stairs. You dashed out of the house and out into the rain, grabbing up the first coat that you came to as you went past the hall stand. You were so excited that you didn't even notice that one of *your* coats was there, but picked a man's coat."

72

"All right," she said, speaking in that same swift, impatient tone of voice, "then what happened?"

"Then," Mason continued, "you ran out into the rain, and there was an automobile parked out in the driveway, but you were too excited to notice the automobile, what kind it was, or whether it was a closed car or a touring car. You just started running. Then a man dashed out of the house behind you, jumped in the automobile, and switched on the headlights. You plunged into the shrubbery because you were afraid he was chasing you.

"The car went on past you down the drive and down the hill, and you started running to follow it, trying to get the license number, because, by that time, you realized the importance of finding out who this man was who had been with your husband when the shot was fired."

"All right," she said. "And then?"

"Still just the way you told it to me. You were afraid to go back to the house alone, and you went to the nearest telephone. Remember that all of that time you didn't know that your husband had been killed. You only knew that you had heard a shot fired, and you didn't know whether it was your husband who had fired the shot and wounded the man who escaped in the automobile, or whether that man had fired the shot at your husband. You didn't know whether the shot had hit, or whether it had missed, whether your husband was wounded, slightly, seriously, or killed, or whether your husband had shot himself while this man was in the room. Can you remember all that?"

"Yes, I think so."

"All right," he said. "That accounts for your reason in calling me. I told you that I would come right out. Remember that you didn't tell me over the telephone a shot had been fired. You simply told me that you were in trouble and afraid and wanted me to come."

"How did it happen that I wanted *you* to come?" she asked. "What excuse is there for that?"

73

"I'm an old friend of yours," he said. "I take it that you and your husband don't go around together much socially."

"No."

"That's fine," Mason said. "You've been calling me by my first name once or twice lately. Begin to do it regularly, particularly when people are around. I'm going to be an old friend of yours and you called me as a friend, not particularly as an attorney."

"I see."

"Now the question is, can you remember all that? Answer!"

"Yes," she said.

He gave the room a quick survey.

"You said you left your purse up here. You'd better find it."

She walked to the desk and opened one of the drawers. The purse was in that. She took it out. "How about the gun?" she asked. "Hadn't we better do something with the gun?"

He followed her eyes, and saw an automatic lying on the floor, almost underneath the desk, where the shadows kept it from being plainly visible.

"No," he said, "that's a break for us. The police may be able to trace this gun, and find out who it belongs to."

She frowned and said, "It seems funny that a man would shoot and then throw the gun down here. We don't know who that gun belongs to. Don't you think we had better do something with it?"

"Do *what* with it?"

"Hide it some place."

"Do that," he said, "and then you *will* have something to explain. Let the police find the gun."

"I've got a lot of confidence in you, Perry," she replied. "But I'd a lot rather have it the other way. Just the dead body here."

"No," he said, shortly. "You can remember everything
I told you?"

"Yes."

He picked up the telephone.

"Police Headquarters," he said.

9

BILL HOFFMAN, HEAD OF THE HOMICIDE SQUAD, WAS A
big, patient man with slow, searching eyes, and a habit of
turning things over and over in his mind before he reached
a definite conclusion.

He sat in the living room on the downstairs floor of
the Belter house and stared through his cigarette smoke at
Perry Mason.

"The papers that we've found," he said, "indicate that
he was the real owner of *Spicy Bits*, the blackmailing sheet
that's been shaking them down during the last five or six
years."

Perry Mason spoke, slowly and cautiously, "I knew
that, Sergeant."

"How long have you known it?" asked Hoffman.

"Not very long."

"How did you find out?"

"That's something I can't tell."

"How did you happen to be here tonight before the
police came?"

"You heard what Mrs. Belter said. That's true. She
called me. She was inclined to think that her husband
might have lost his head, and shot the man who was calling

on him. She didn't know what had happened, and was afraid to go and find out."

"Why was she afraid?" asked Hoffman.

Perry Mason shrugged his shoulders.

"You've seen the man," he said, "and you know the type of a man it would take to run *Spicy Bits*. I would say, offhand, that he was rather hard-boiled. He might not be a perfect gentleman or very chivalrous in dealing with women-folks."

Bill Hoffman turned the matter over in his mind.

"Well," he said, "we can tell a lot more when we've traced that gun."

"Can you trace it?" asked Mason.

"I think so. The numbers are on it."

"Yes," Mason said, "I saw them when they took down the numbers. A 32-caliber Colt automatic, eh?"

"That's the gun," said Hoffman.

There was a period of silence. Hoffman smoked meditatively. Perry Mason sat perfectly still without so much as moving a muscle, the pose of a man who is either absolutely relaxed, or else is afraid to give way to the slightest motion for fear that it will betray him.

Once or twice Bill Hoffman raised his placid eyes and looked at Perry Mason. Finally Hoffman said, "There's something funny about this whole thing, Mason. I don't know just how to explain it."

"Well," said Mason, "it's your business. I usually get in on the murder cases long after the police have finished. This is a new experience for me."

Hoffman flashed him a glance.

"Yes," he said, "it *is* rather unusual for an attorney to be on the ground before the police get there, isn't it?"

"Yes," said Mason, noncommittally, "I think I can agree with you upon that word 'unusual.' "

Hoffman smoked awhile in silence.

"Located the nephew yet?" asked Mason.

"No," said Hoffman. "We've covered most of the places

76

where he usually hangs out. We crossed his trail earlier in the evening. He'd been out with some jane at a night club. We've located her all right. She said that he left her before midnight. About eleven-fifteen she thinks it was."

Suddenly there sounded the noise of a motor pounding up the drive. The rain had ceased, and the moon was breaking through the clouds.

Above the noise of the motor could be heard a steady thump . . . thump . . . thump . . . thump.

The car came to a stop, and a horn blared.

"Now what the devil?" said Bill Hoffman, and got slowly to his feet.

Perry Mason had his head cocked on one side, listening. "Sounds like a flat," he said.

Bill Hoffman moved toward the door, and Perry Mason followed along behind him.

Sergeant Hoffman opened the front door.

There were four or five police cars parked in the driveway. The car that had just driven up was on the outside of the circle of parked cars. It was a roadster with side curtains up. A vague form at the wheel was staring at the house. The white blur of his face could be seen through the side curtains of the car. He was holding one hand on the horn which kept up a steady, incessant racket.

Sergeant Hoffman stepped out into the light on the porch, and the noise of the horn ceased.

The door of the roadster opened, and a voice called in thick accents:

"Digley. I got . . . flat tire . . . can't change . . . don't dare bend over . . . don't feel well. You come fixsh car . . . fixsh tire."

Perry Mason remarked casually, "That probably will be the nephew, Carl Griffin. We'll see what he has to say."

Bill Hoffman grunted. "If I'm any judge at this distance, he won't be able to say much."

Together they moved toward the car.

The young man crawled out from behind the steering

wheel, felt vaguely with a groping foot for the step of the roadster, and lurched forward. He would have fallen, had it not been for his hand which caught and held one of the supports of the top. He stood there, weaving uncertainly back and forth.

"Got flat tire," he said. "Want Digley . . . you're not Digley. There's two of you . . . not either one of you Digley. Who the hell are you? What you want thish time of night? 'Snot a nicesh time night for men to come pay call."

Bill Hoffman moved forward.

"You're drunk," he said.

The man leered at him with owlish scrutiny.

"Course I'm drunk . . . wash schpose I shtayed out for? Course I'm drunk."

Hoffman said patiently: "Are you Carl Griffin?"

"Coursh I'm Carl Griffin."

"All right," said Bill Hoffman. "You'd better snap out of it. Your uncle has been murdered."

There was a moment of silence. The man who held to the top of the roadster shook his head two or three times, as though trying to shake away some mental fog which gripped him.

When he spoke, his voice was more crisp.

"What are you talking about?" he asked.

"Your uncle," said the Sergeant. "That is, I presume he's your uncle, George C. Belter. He was murdered an hour or an hour and a half ago."

The reek of whiskey enveloped the man. He was struggling to get his self-possession. He took two or three deep breaths, and then said, "You're drunk."

Sergeant Hoffman smiled. "No, Griffin, *we're* not drunk," he said, patiently. "You're the one that's drunk. You've been out going places and doing things. You'd better come in the house and see if you can pull yourself together."

"Did you say 'murdered'?" asked the young man.

78

"That's what I said—murdered," repeated Sergeant Hoffman.

The young man started walking toward the house. He was holding his head very erect with his shoulders back.

"If he was murdered," he said, "it was that damned woman that did it."

"Who do you mean?" asked Sergeant Hoffman.

"That baby-faced bitch he married," said the young man.

Hoffman took the young man's arm and turned back to Perry Mason.

"Mason," he said, "would you mind switching off the motor on that car and turning off the lights?"

Carl Griffin paused, and turned unsteadily back.

"Change tire, too," he said, "right front tire—it's been flat for miles and miles . . . better change it."

Perry Mason switched off the motor and lights, slammed the door on the roadster, and walked rapidly to catch up with the pair ahead of him.

He was in time to open the front door for Bill Hoffman and the man on his arm.

Seen under the light in the hallway, Carl Griffin was a rather good-looking young man with a face which was flushed with drink, marked with dissipation. His eyes were red and bleary, but there was a certain innate dignity about him, a stamp of breeding which made itself manifest in the manner in which he tried to adjust himself to the emergency.

Bill Hoffman faced him, studied him carefully.

"Do you suppose that you could sober up enough to talk with us, Griffin?" he asked.

Griffin nodded. "Just a minute . . . I'll be all right."

He pushed away from Sergeant Hoffman and staggered toward a lavatory which opened off the reception room on the lower floor.

Hoffman looked at Mason.

"He's pretty drunk," said Mason.

"Sure he's drunk," Hoffman replied, "but it isn't like an amateur getting drunk. He's used to it. He drove the car all the way up here with the roads wet, and with a tire flat."

"Yes," agreed Mason, "he could drive the car all right."

"Apparently no love lost between him and Eva Belter," Sergeant Hoffman pointed out.

"You mean what he said about her?" asked Mason.

"Sure," said Hoffman. "What else would I mean?"

"He was drunk," Mason said. "You wouldn't suspect a woman on account of the thoughtless remark of a drunken man, would you?"

"Sure, he was drunk," said Hoffman, "and he piloted the car up here, all right. Maybe he could think straight even if he was drunk."

Perry Mason shrugged his shoulders.

"Have it your own way," he said, carelessly.

From the bathroom came the sounds of violent retchings.

"I'll bet you he sobers up," remarked Sergeant Hoffman, watching Perry Mason with wary eyes, "and says the same things about the woman when he's sober."

"I'll bet you he's drunk as a lord, no matter whether he *seems* to be sober or not," snapped Mason. "Some of these fellows are pretty deceptive when it comes to carrying their booze. They get so they can act as sober as judges, but they haven't very much of an idea what they're doing or saying."

Bill Hoffman looked at him with a suggestion of a twinkle in his eyes.

"Sort of discounting in advance what ever it may be that he's going to say, eh, Mason?"

"I didn't say that."

Hoffman laughed.

"No," he said, "you didn't *say* it. Not in exactly those words."

"How about getting him some black coffee?" asked

Mason. "I think I can find the kitchen and put some coffee on."

"The housekeeper should be out there," Hoffman said. "I don't want to offend you, Mason, but I really want to talk to this man alone, anyway. I don't know exactly what your status in this case is. You seem to be a friend of the family and a lawyer both."

"That's all right," Mason agreed readily enough. "I understand your position, Sergeant. I happen to be out here, and I'm sticking around."

Hoffman nodded. "You'll find the housekeeper in the kitchen, I think. Mrs. Veitch, her name is. We had her and her daughter upstairs questioning them. Go on out there and see if they can scare up some coffee. Get lots of black coffee. I think that the boys upstairs would like it as well as this chap, Griffin."

"Okay," Mason said. He went through the folding doors from the dining room, then pushed through a swinging door into a serving pantry, and from there into the kitchen.

The kitchen was enormous, well lit, and well equipped. Two women were seated at a table. They were in straight-backed chairs, and were sitting close to each other. They had been talking in low tones when Perry Mason stepped into the room, and they ceased their conversation abruptly and looked up.

One of them was a woman in the late forties, with hair that was shot with gray, deep-set, lack-luster, black eyes that seemed to have been pulled into her face by invisible strings that had worked the eyes so far back into the sockets it was hard to tell their expression. They hid from sight back in the shadowed hollows. She had a long face, a thin, firm mouth, and high cheek bones. She was dressed in black.

The other woman was very much younger, not over twenty-two or three. Her hair was jet black and glossy. Her eyes were a snapping black, and their brightness emphasized the dullness of the deep-sunken eyes of the older woman. Her lips were full and very red. Her face had received careful attention with rouge and powder. The eyebrows were thin, black and arched, the eyelashes long.

"You're Mrs. Veitch?" asked Perry Mason, addressing the older woman.

She nodded in tight-lipped silence.

The girl at her side spoke in a rich, throaty voice.

"I'm Norma Veitch, her daughter. What is it you wanted? Mother's all upset."

"Yes, I know," apologized Mason. "I wondered if we could get some coffee. Carl Griffin has just come home, and I think he's going to need it. And there's a bunch of men working on the case upstairs who will want some."

Norma Veitch got to her feet. "Why, I guess so. It's all right, isn't it, Mother?" she asked.

She glanced at the older woman, and the older woman nodded her head once more.

"I'll get it, Mother," said Norma Veitch.

"No," said the older woman, speaking in a voice that was as dry as the rustling of corn husks. "I'll get it. You don't know where things are."

She pushed back her chair and walked across the kitchen to a cupboard. She slid back a door and took down a huge coffee percolator and a can of coffee. Her face was absolutely expressionless, but she moved as though she were very tired.

She was flat-chested and flat-hipped and walked with springless steps. Her entire manner was that of dejection.

The girl turned to Mason and flashed him a smile from her full red lips.

"You're a detective?" she asked.

Mason shook his head. "No," he said, "I'm the man that was here with Mrs. Belter. I'm the one that called the police."

Norma Veitch said, "Oh, yes. I heard something about you."

Mason turned to the mother.

"I can make the coffee all right, Mrs. Veitch, if you don't feel able."

"No," she said in that same dry, expressionless voice. "I can make it all right."

She poured coffee into the container, put water in the percolator, walked over to the gas stove, lit the gas, looked at the percolator for a moment, then walked with her peculiar, flat-footed gait back to the chair, sat down, folded her hands on her lap, and lowered her eyes so that she was staring at the top of the table. She continued to stare there in fixed intensity.

Norma Veitch looked up at Perry Mason. "My," she said, "it was horrible. Wasn't it?"

Mason nodded, remarked casually, "You didn't hear the shot, I presume?"

The girl shook her head.

"No, I was sound asleep. In fact, I didn't wake up until after the officers came. They got Mother up, and I guess they didn't know that I was sleeping in the adjoining room. They wanted to look through Mother's room while she was upstairs, I guess. Anyway, the first thing I knew, I woke up and there was a man standing by the bed looking down at me."

She lowered her eyes and tittered slightly.

One gathered that she had not found the experience unpleasant.

"What happened?" asked Mason.

"They acted as though they thought they had discovered the nigger in the woodpile," she said. "They made me put on clothes and wouldn't even let me out of their sight while I was dressing. They took me upstairs, and gave me what they call a third degree, I guess."

"What did you tell them?" asked Mason.

"Told them the truth," she said, "that I went to bed and went to sleep, and woke up to find somebody staring down at me." She seemed rather pleased as she added, "They didn't believe me."

83

Her mother sat at the table, hands folded on her lap, eyes staring steadily in fixed intensity at the center of the table.

"And you didn't hear anything, or see anything?" asked Perry Mason.

"Not a thing."

"Have you any ideas about it?"

She shook her head.

"None that would bear repeating."

He glanced at her sharply.

"Have you any that wouldn't bear repeating?" he inquired.

She nodded her head.

"Of course, I've only been around here a week or so, but in that time . . ."

"Normal!" said her mother, in a voice which had suddenly lost its dry huskiness and cracked like the lash of a whip.

The girl lapsed into abrupt silence.

Perry Mason glanced at the older woman. She had not so much as raised her eyes from the table when she spoke.

"Did *you* hear anything, Mrs. Veitch?" he asked.

"I am a servant. I hear nothing, and I see nothing."

"Rather commendable for one who is a servant, as far as minor matters are concerned," he observed, "but I think you will find the law has ideas of its own upon the matter, and that you will be required to see and to hear."

"No," she said, without so much as moving a muscle of her head. "I saw nothing."

"And heard nothing?"

"And heard nothing."

Perry Mason scowled. Somehow he sensed that the woman was concealing something.

"Did you answer those questions in just that way when you were questioned upstairs?" he asked.

"I think," she said, "the coffee is about ready to start

percolating. You can turn the fire down as soon as it does, so that it doesn't boil over."

Mason turned to the coffee. The percolator was specially designed to heat a maximum of water in a small amount of time, and the fire under it was a blue flame of terrific heat. Steam was commencing to rise from the water.

"I'll watch the coffee," he said, "but I *am* interested to know whether or not you answered the questions in exactly that way when you were upstairs."

"What way?" she countered.

"The way you answered them here."

"I told them the same thing," she said, "that I saw nothing and heard nothing."

Norma Veitch giggled. "That's her story," she said, "and she sticks to it."

The mother snapped, "Norma!"

Mason stared at them both, his thoughtful face apparently absolutely placid. Only his eyes were hard and calculating.

"You know," he said, "I'm a lawyer. If you have anything to confide in me, now would make an excellent time."

"Yes," said Mrs. Veitch, tonelessly.

"How's that?" asked Perry Mason.

"I merely agreed," she said, "that this would be an excellent time."

There was a moment of silence.

"Well?" said Mason.

"But I have nothing to confide," she said, her eyes still fixed on the table top.

At that moment, the percolator commenced to bubble. Mason turned down the fire.

"I'll get some cups and saucers," said Norma, jumping to her feet.

Mrs. Veitch said, "Sit down, Norma. I'll do it." She pushed back her chair, walked to one of the cupboards,

85

and took down some cups and saucers. "They'll drink out of these."

"Mother," said Norma, "those are the cups and saucers that are kept for the chauffeurs and servants."

"These are police officers," said Mrs. Veitch. "They're just the same."

"No, they aren't, Mother," said Norma.

"I'm doing this," said Mrs. Veitch. "You know what the master would have said had he been alive. He'd have given them nothing."

Norma Veitch said, "Well, he isn't alive. Mrs. Belter is going to be the one that runs things."

Mrs. Veitch turned and looked steadily at her daughter from those deep-set, lack-luster eyes.

"Don't be too sure that she is," she said.

Perry Mason poured some of the coffee into the cups, and then poured it back through the coffee container in the percolator. When he had poured it through the second time, it was black and steaming.

"Get me a tray," he said, "and I'll take in a couple of cups to Sergeant Hoffman and Carl Griffin. You can serve coffee to the others upstairs."

Wordlessly, she secured him a tray. Perry Mason poured three cups of coffee, picked up the tray, and walked into the dining room, through it into the sitting room.

Sergeant Hoffman was standing, his shoulders thrown back, his head thrust forward, feet wide apart.

Plumped down in one of the chairs, his face flushed and his eyes very red, was Carl Griffin.

Sergeant Hoffman was talking as Perry Mason brought in the coffee.

"That wasn't the way you talked about her when you first came in," Sergeant Hoffman said.

"I was drunk then," said Griffin.

Hoffman stared at him. "Many times a person tells the

truth when he's drunk and conceals his feelings when he's sober," he remarked.

Carl Griffin raised his eyebrows in an expression of well-bred surprise.

"Indeed?" he observed. "I'd never noticed it."

Sergeant Hoffman heard Mason behind him, whirled, and grinned as he saw the steaming cups of coffee.

"Okay, Mason," he said, "that's going to come in pretty handy. Drink one of these, Griffin, and you'll feel better."

Griffin nodded. "It looks good, but I feel all right now."

Mason handed him a cup of coffee.

"Do you know anything about a will?" asked Sergeant Hoffman, abruptly.

"I'd rather not answer that, if you don't mind, Sergeant," Griffin answered.

Hoffman took himself a cup of coffee. "It happens that I do mind," he commented. "I want you to answer that question."

"Yes, there's a will," Griffin admitted.

"Where is it?" asked Hoffman.

"I don't know."

"How do you know there is one?"

"He showed it to me."

"Does the property all go to his wife?"

Griffin shook his head.

"I don't think anything goes to her," he said, "except the sum of five thousand dollars."

Sergeant Hoffman raised his eyebrows, and whistled.

"That," he said, "puts a different aspect on it."

"Different aspect on what?" asked Griffin.

"On the whole situation," said Hoffman. "She was kept here practically dependent on him, and upon his continuing to live. The minute he died, she was put out with virtually nothing."

Griffin volunteered a statement by way of explanation. "I don't think they were very congenial."

Sergeant Hoffman said, musingly, "That's not the point. Usually in any of these cases, we have to look for a motive."

Mason grinned at Sergeant Hoffman.

"Are you insinuating that Mrs. Belter fired the shot which killed her husband?" he asked, as though the entire idea were humorous.

"I was making a routine investigation, Mason, in order to find out who *might* have killed him. In such cases, we always look for a motive. We try to find out any one who would have benefited by his death."

"In that case," Griffin remarked, soberly, "I presume that *I'll* come under suspicion."

"How do you mean?" asked Hoffman.

"Under the terms of the will," said Griffin slowly, "I take virtually all of the estate. I don't know as it's any particular secret. I think that Uncle George had more affection for me than he did for any one else in the world. That is, he had as much affection for me as he could have, considering his disposition. I doubt if he was capable of having affection for any one."

"How did you feel toward him?" asked Hoffman.

"I respected his mind," Carl Griffin replied, choosing his words carefully, "and I think I appreciated something of his disposition. He lived a life that was very much apart, because he had a mind which was very impatient of all subterfuges and hypocrisies."

"Why did that condemn him to live apart?" asked Sergeant Hoffman.

Griffin made a slight motion with his shoulders.

"If you had a mind like that," he said, "you wouldn't need to ask the question. The man had wonderful intellectual capacity. He had the ability to see through people and to penetrate sham and hypocrisy. He was the type of a man who never made any friends. He was so thoroughly

88

self-reliant that he didn't have to lean on any one, and, therefore, he hadn't any ground for establishing friendship. His sole inclination was to fight. He fought the world and everyone in it."

"Evidently he didn't fight you," said Sergeant Hoffman.

"No," admitted Griffin, "he didn't fight me, because he knew that I didn't give a damn about him or his money. I didn't lick his boots, and, on the other hand, I didn't double-cross him. I told him what I thought, and I shot fair with him."

Sergeant Hoffman narrowed his eyes. "Who did double-cross him?" he asked.

"Why, what do you mean?"

"You said you didn't double-cross him, so he liked you."

"That's right."

"And there was an emphasis on the pronoun you used."

"I didn't mean it that way."

"How about his wife? Didn't he like her?"

"I don't know. He didn't discuss his wife with me."

"Did *she* double-cross him?" demanded Sergeant Hoffman.

"How should I know that?"

Sergeant Hoffman stared at the young man. "You sure know how to keep things to yourself," he mused, "but if you won't talk, you won't talk, so that's all there is to it."

"But I'll talk, Sergeant," protested Griffin, "I'll tell you everything I can."

Sergeant Hoffman sighed and said, "Can you tell me exactly where you were when the murder was committed?"

A flush came over Griffin's face.

"I'm sorry, Sergeant," he said, "but I can't."

"Why?" asked Sergeant Hoffman.

"Because," said Griffin, "in the first place, I don't know when the murder was committed, and in the second place, I wouldn't know where I was. I'm afraid I'd been making quite an evening of it. I was out with a young woman earlier in the evening, and after I left her I went to a few night spots on my own. When I started home, I had that damned flat tire and I knew I was too drunk to change it. I couldn't find a garage that was open, and it was raining, so I just fought the car along over the road. It must have taken me hours to get here."

"The tire was pretty well chewed to pieces," remarked Sergeant Hoffman. "And, by the way, did any one else know of your uncle's will? Had any one else seen it?"

"Oh, yes," Griffin answered, "my lawyer saw it."

"Oh," said Sergeant Hoffman, "so *you* had a lawyer, too, did you?"

"Of course I had a lawyer. Why wouldn't I?"

"Who is he?" asked Hoffman.

"Arthur Atwood. He's got offices in the Mutual Building."

Sergeant Hoffman turned to Mason. "I don't know him. Do you know him, Mason?"

"Yes," Mason said, "I've met him once or twice. He's a baldheaded chap, who used to do some personal injury work. They say he always settles his cases out of court and always gets a good settlement."

"How did you happen to see the will in the presence of your lawyer?" pressed Sergeant Hoffman. "It's not usual for a man to call in the beneficiary under his will, together with his lawyer, in order to show them how the will is made, is it?"

Griffin pressed his lips together. "*That's* something that you'll have to ask my attorney about. I simply can't go into it. It's rather a complicated matter and one that I would prefer not to discuss."

Sergeant Hoffman snapped. "All right, let's forget about that stuff. Now go ahead and tell me what it was."

"What do you mean?" asked Griffin.

Bill Hoffman turned around so that he was squarely facing the young man, and looked down at him. His jaw was thrust slightly forward, and his patient eyes were suddenly hard.

"I mean just this, Griffin," he said, slowly and ominously, "you can't pull that stuff. You're trying to protect somebody, or trying to be a gentleman, or something of the sort. It won't go. You either tell me what you know here and now, or else you go to jail as a material witness."

Griffin's face flushed. "I say," he protested, "isn't that rather steep?"

"I don't give a damn how steep it is," Hoffman said. "This is a murder case, and you're sitting here trying to play button, button, who's got the button with me. Now come on, and kick through. What was said at that time, and how did it happen that the will was exhibited to you and to your lawyer?"

Griffin spoke reluctantly. "You understand that I'm telling you this under protest?"

"Sure," said Hoffman, "go ahead and tell me. What is it?"

"Well," Griffin said slowly and with evident reluctance, "I've intimated that Uncle George and his wife weren't on the best of terms. Uncle George had an idea that perhaps she was going to bring a suit against him for divorce in the event she could get the sort of evidence she wanted. Uncle George and I had some business dealings together, you know, and one time when Atwood and myself were discussing a business matter with him, he suddenly brought this other thing up. It was embarrassing to me, and I didn't want to go ahead and discuss it, but Atwood looked at it just the way any lawyer would."

Carl Griffin turned to Perry Mason. "I think you understand how that is, sir. I understand you're an attorney."

Bill Hoffman kept his eyes on Griffin's face. "Never mind him. Go on. What happened?"

"Well," said Griffin, "Uncle George made that single crack about him and his wife not being on the best of terms, and he held out a paper which he had in his hands, and which seemed to be all in his handwriting, and asked Mr. Atwood as a lawyer, if a will made entirely in the handwriting of the person who wrote it, was good without witnesses, or whether it needed to be witnessed. He said that he'd made his will, and that he thought there might be a contest because he wasn't leaving much of his property to his wife. In fact, I believe he mentioned the sum of five thousand dollars, and he said that the bulk of the estate was to go to me."

"You didn't read the will?" asked Sergeant Hoffman.

"Well, not exactly. No, not in the way that you'd pick it up and look it through, word for word. I glanced at it, and saw that it was in his handwriting, and heard what he had to say about it. Atwood, I think, read it more carefully."

"All right," said Hoffman, "go ahead. Then what?"

"That was all," said Griffin.

"No, it wasn't," Hoffman insisted. "What else?"

Griffin shrugged his shoulders. "Oh, well," he said, "he went on to say something else, the way a man will sometimes. I didn't pay any attention to it."

"Never mind that line of hooey," pressed Hoffman. "What was it he said?"

"He said," blurted Griffin, his face coloring, "that he wanted it fixed so that if anything happened to him, his wife wouldn't profit by it. He said that he wouldn't put it past her to get his fortune by expediting his end, in the event she found she couldn't get a good slice of it through divorce proceedings. Now you know everything I know. And I don't think it's any of your damned business. I'm telling you this under protest, and I don't like your attitude."

"Never mind the side comments," Hoffman said. "I presume that accounts for your comment when you were drunk, and right after you had first heard about the murder. To the effect that . . ."

Griffin interrupted, holding up his hand.

"Please, Sergeant," he said, "don't bring that up. If I said it, I don't remember it, and I certainly didn't mean it."

Perry Mason said, "Maybe you didn't mean it, but you certainly managed . . ."

Sergeant Hoffman whirled on him.

"That'll do from you, Mason!" he said. "I'm running this. You're here as an audience, and you can keep quiet, or get out!"

"You're not frightening me a damned bit, Sergeant," Mason said. "I'm here in the house of Mrs. Eva Belter, as attorney for Mrs. Eva Belter, and I hear a man making statements which are bound to be damaging to her reputation, if not otherwise. I am going to see that those statements are substantiated or withdrawn."

The look of patience had entirely vanished from Hoffman's eyes. He stared at Mason moodily.

"Well," he said, "stick up for your rights if you want to. And I don't know but what *you've* got some explaining to do at that. It's a damn funny thing that the police come here and find a murder, with you and a woman sitting here talking things over. And it's a damn funny thing, that when a woman discovers her husband has been murdered, she goes and rings up her attorney, before she does anything else."

Mason remarked hotly, "That's not a fair statement, and you know it. I'm a friend of hers."

"So it would seem," said Sergeant Hoffman, dryly.

Mason planted his feet wide apart and squared his shoulders. "Now, let's get this straight," he said. "I'm representing Eva Belter. There's no reason on God's green earth for throwing any mud at her. George Belter wasn't worth a damned thing to her dead. He was, to this guy. This guy comes drifting in with an alibi that won't stand up and starts taking cracks at my client."

Griffin protested hotly.

93

Mason kept staring at Sergeant Hoffman. "By God, you can't convict a woman with a lot of loose talk. It takes a jury to do that. And a jury can't convict her until she's proven guilty beyond a reasonable doubt."

The big sergeant looked at Perry Mason searchingly.

"And you're looking for a reasonable doubt, Mason?"

Mason pointed his finger at Carl Griffin.

"Just so *you* won't shoot off your face too much, young fellow," he said, "if my client ever goes before a jury, don't think I'm dumb enough to overlook the advantage I can get from dragging you and this will into the case."

"You mean you think *he's* guilty of this murder?" asked Sergeant Hoffman, coaxingly.

"I'm not a detective," said Mason. "I'm a lawyer. I know that the jury can't convict anybody as long as they've got a reasonable doubt. And if you start framing anything on my client, there sits my reasonable doubt right in that chair!"

Hoffman nodded.

"About what I expected," he said. "I shouldn't have let you sit in on this thing in the first place. Now you can get out!"

"I'm going," Mason told him.

10

IT WAS NEARLY THREE O'CLOCK IN THE MORNING WHEN Perry Mason got Paul Drake on the telephone.

"Paul," he said, "I've got another job for you, and it's

a rush job. Have you got any more men you can put on the case?"

Paul's voice was sleepy.

"Gee, guy," he said, "ain't you ever satisfied?"

"Listen," said Mason, "wake up and snap out of it. I've got a job that's got to be done in a hurry, and you've got to beat the police to it."

"How the devil can I beat the police to it?" asked Paul Drake.

"You can," Mason told him, "because I happen to know that you've got access to certain records. You represented the Merchants Protective Association that kept duplicate records of all firearms sold in the city. Now, I want a Colt 32-automatic placed, with number 127337. The police are going to dig into it as a matter of routine, along with a lot of fingerprint stuff, and it'll probably be some time in the morning before they feed it through the mill. They know it's important, but they don't figure there's any great hurry about it. What I want you to do is to get the dope in advance of the police. I've simply got to beat them to it."

"What happened with the gun?" asked Paul Drake.

"A guy got shot with it once, right through the heart," said Perry Mason.

Drake whistled. "Is that in connection with the other stuff I've been looking up?"

"I don't think so," Mason said, "but the police may. I've got to be in a position to protect my client. I want you to get the information, and get it before the police do."

"Okay," said Drake. "Where can I call you back?"

"You can't," Mason said. "I'll call you."

"When?"

"I'll call you again in an hour."

"I won't have it by then," protested Drake. "I couldn't."

"You've got to," Mason insisted, "and I'll call you anyway. Good-by." And he hung up the telephone. He then called the number of Harrison Burke's residence. There was no answer. He called Della Street's number, and her sleepy "Hello" came over the line, almost at once.

"This is Perry Mason, Della," he said. "Wake up and get the sleepy dirt out of your eyes. We've got work to do."

"What time is it?" she asked.

"Around three o'clock, or quarter past."

"Okay," she said. "What is it?"

"You awake all right?"

"Of course I'm awake. What do you think I'm doing, talking in my sleep?"

"Never mind the cracks," he told her, "this is serious. Can you get some clothes on and get down to the office right away? I'll order a taxi to be out at the house by the time you get dressed."

"I'm dressing right now," she answered. "Do I take time to make myself pretty, or do I just put on some clothes?"

"Better make yourself pretty," he answered, "but don't take too long doing it."

"Right now," she said, and hung up on him.

Mason telephoned a taxi company to send a cab out to her apartment. Then he left the all night drug store, from which he had been telephoning, got in his car, and drove rapidly to his office.

He switched on the lights, pulled down the shades, and started pacing the floor.

Back and forth, back and forth he paced, his hands behind his back, his head thrust forward, and slightly bowed. There was something of the appearance of a caged tiger in his manner. He seemed impatient, and yet it was a controlled impatience. A fighter who was cornered, savage, who didn't dare make a false move.

A key sounded in the door, and Della Street walked in.

"Morning, chief," she said. "You sure do keep hours!"

96

He beckoned to her to come in and sit down. "This," he said, "is the start of a busy day."

"What is it?" she asked, looking at him with troubled eyes.

"Murder."

"We're just representing a client?" she inquired.

"I don't know. We may be mixed up in it."

"Mixed up in it?"

"Yes."

"It's that woman," she said savagely.

He shook his head impatiently. "I wish you'd get over those ideas, Della."

"That's right just the same," she persisted. "I knew there was something about her. I knew there was trouble that was going to follow that woman around. I never did trust her."

"Okay," Mason said wearily. "Now forget that, and get your instructions. I don't know what's going to happen here, and you may have to carry on if anything happens that I can't keep the ball rolling."

"What do you mean," she asked, "that you can't?"

"Never mind about that."

"But I do mind," she said, eyes wide with apprehension. "You're in danger."

He ignored the remark. "This woman came to us as Eva Griffin. I tried to follow her, and couldn't make it stick. Later on, I started a fight with *Spicy Bits,* and tried to find out who was really back of the sheet. It turned out to be a man named Belter who lived out on Elmwood Drive. You'll read about the place and the chap in the morning papers. I went out to see Belter and found he was a tough customer. While I was there, I ran into his wife. And she was none other than our client. Her real name is Eva Belter."

"What was she trying to do?" asked Della Street. "Double-cross you?"

"No," said Mason. "She was in a jam. She'd been places

97

with a man, and her husband was on her back trail. He didn't know who the woman was. It was the man he was after. But he was exposing the man through the scandal sheet, and eventually the identity of the woman would have come out."

"Who is this man?" asked Della Street.

"Harrison Burke," he said, slowly.

She arched her eyebrows and was silent.

Mason lit a cigarette.

"What does Harrison Burke have to say about it?" she asked after a little while.

Perry Mason made a gesture with his hands.

"He was the guy that kicked through with the money in the envelope; the coin that came into the office this afternoon by messenger."

"Oh."

There was silence for a minute or two. Both were thinking.

"Well," she said at length, "go on. What am I going to read about in the papers tomorrow?"

He spoke in a monotone. "I went to bed, and Eva Belter called me sometime after midnight. Around twelve thirty, I guess it was. It was raining to beat the band. She wanted me to come out and pick her up at a drug store. She said she was in trouble. I went out, and she told me that some man had been having an argument with her husband and shot him."

"Did she know the man?" Della Street inquired softly.

"No," said Mason, "she didn't. She didn't see him. She only heard his voice."

"Did she know the voice?"

"She thought she did."

"Who did she think it was?"

"Me."

The girl looked at him steadily, her eyes not changing their expression in the least.

"Was it?"

"No. I was at home, in bed."

"Can you prove it?" she asked, tonelessly.

"Good Lord," he said, impatiently. "I don't take an alibi to bed with me!"

"The lousy little double-crosser!" More calmly she asked, "Then what happened?"

"We went out there, and found her husband dead. A 32-Colt automatic. I got the number of it. One shot, right through the heart. He'd been taking a bath, and somebody shot him."

Della Street's eyes widened. "Then she got you out there before she notified the police?"

"Exactly," said Mason. "The police don't like that."

The girl's face was white. She sucked in her breath to say something, but thought better of it and remained silent.

Perry Mason went on, in his same monotone: "I had a run-in with Sergeant Hoffman. There's a nephew out there that I don't like. He's too much of a gentleman. The housekeeper's concealing something, and I think her daughter is lying. I didn't get a chance to talk with the other servants. The police held me downstairs while they made the investigation upstairs. But I had a chance to look around a little bit before the police got there."

"How bad was your trouble with Sergeant Hoffman?" she asked.

"Bad enough," he said, "the way things are."

"You mean you have to stick up for your client?" she asked, her eyes suspiciously moist. "What's going to happen next?"

"I don't know. I think that the housekeeper is going to crack. They evidently haven't gone after her very hard yet. But they will. I think she knows something. I don't know what it is. I'm not even sure that Eva Belter gave me the full facts of the case."

"If she did," said Della Street, savagely, "it's the first time since she's been in here that she hasn't concealed something, and lied about something else. And that busi-

99

ness of dragging you into it! Bah! The cat! I could kill her!"

Mason waved his hand, deprecatingly. "Never mind that. I'm in this now."

"Does Harrison Burke know about this murder business?" she asked.

"I tried to get him on the telephone. He's out."

"What a sweet time for *him* to be out!" she exclaimed.

Mason smiled wearily. "Isn't it?"

They looked at each other.

Della Street took a quick breath, started speaking impulsively.

"Look here," she said, "you're letting this woman get you in a funny position. You had words with this man who was killed. You were fighting his paper, and when you fight, you don't do it gently. That woman trapped you to get you out there. She wanted you to be there when the police came. She's getting ready to throw you to the wolves, if it looks as though her precious hands were going to get soiled. Now are you going to let her get away with that?"

"Not if I can help it," he said, "but I won't go back on her until I have to."

Della Street's face was white, her lips drawn into a thin, firm line. "She's a . . ." she said, and stopped.

"She's a client," insisted Perry Mason, "and she's paying well."

"Paying well for what? To have you represent her in a blackmail case? Or to take a rap for murder?"

There were tears in her eyes.

"Mr. Mason," she said, "please don't be so damned big hearted. Keep on the outside of this thing, and let them go ahead and do whatever they want to. You simply act as an attorney and come into the case as a lawyer."

His voice was patient. "It's pretty late for that now, isn't it, Della?"

"No, it isn't. You keep out of it!"

100

He smiled patiently. "She's a client, Della."

"That's all right," she said, "*after* you get to court. You can sit back and see what happens at the trial."

He shook his head. "No, Della, the District Attorney doesn't wait until he gets to court. His representatives are out there right now, talking with the witnesses and putting the words in Carl Griffin's mouth that will become newspaper headlines tomorrow and damaging testimony by the time the case comes to trial."

She recognized the futility of further argument.

"You think they're going to arrest the woman?" she asked.

"I don't know *what* they're going to do," he said.

"Have they found a motive?"

"No," he said, "they haven't found a motive. They started looking for the conventional ones, and they didn't pan out, so that stopped them. But when they find out about this other business, they'll have a motive already made to order."

"Are they going to find out about it?" she asked.

"They're bound to."

Della Street's eyes suddenly widened. "Do you think," she said, "it was Harrison Burke? The man who was out there when the shot was fired?"

"I've tried to get Harrison Burke on the telephone," he said, "and haven't been able to. Aside from that I'm not even thinking. Go on out and get on the telephone. Try him again. Keep trying his house at ten minute intervals until you get him, or get somebody."

"Okay," she said.

"Also, ring up Paul Drake. He'll probably be at his office. If he isn't, try him on that emergency telephone number we've got. He's doing some work for me on this."

She was once more merely a secretary. "Yes, Mr. Mason," she said, and went into the other office.

Perry Mason resumed his pacing of the floor.

After a few minutes, his telephone rang.

He picked up the receiver.

"Paul Drake," said Della Street's voice.

Paul Drake's voice said, "Hello, Perry."

"Have you got anything?" Mason asked.

"Yes, I got a lucky break on that gun business, and I can give you the dope on it."

"Your line's all clear? There's nobody listening?"

"No," said Drake, "it's okay."

"All right," Mason said, "hand it to me."

"I don't suppose you care anything about where the gun was jobbed or who the dealer was?" asked Drake. "What you want is the name of the purchaser."

"That's right."

"All right, your gun was finally purchased by a man named Pete Mitchell, who gave his address as thirteen twenty-two West Sixty-ninth Street."

"All right," said Mason, "have you got any dope on the other angle of the case? About Frank Locke?"

"No, I haven't been able to get a report from our southern agency yet. I've traced him back to a southern state, Georgia it was, and the trail seems to go haywire there. It looks as though that's where he changed his name."

"That's fine," Mason said. "That's where he had his trouble. How about the rest of it? Do you get anything on him?"

"I've got a line on the jane at the Wheelright Hotel," Drake said. "It's a girl named Esther Linten. She lives there at the Wheelright, has room nine-forty-six, by the month."

"What does she do?" asked Mason. "Did you find that out?"

"Anybody she can, I guess," Drake told him. "We can't get very much of a line on her as yet, but give us a little time, and let me get some sleep. A guy can't be every place at once, and work without sleep."

"You'll get used to it after a while," Mason told him,

grinning, "particularly if you keep working on this case. You stay there in the office for five minutes. I'll call you back."

"Okay," sighed Drake, and hung up.

Perry Mason went out to the outer office.

"Della," he said, "do you remember when all of the political stuff was going around a couple of years ago? We made a file for some of the letters?"

"Yes," she said, "there's a file 'Political Letters.' I didn't know what you saved them for."

"Connections," he said. "You'll find a 'Burke-for-Congress-Club' letter some place in there. Get it for me, and make it snappy."

She made a dive for the battery of files which lined one side of the office.

Perry Mason sat on the corner of her desk and watched her. Only his eyes showed the white-hot concentration of thought which was covering a dozen different angles of a complicated problem.

She came to him with a letter.

"That's fine," he said.

Printed in a column on the right hand margin was a list of vice presidents of the "Burke-for-Congress-Club." There were more than a hundred names in fine print.

Mason squinted his eyes and read down the column. Every time he passed over a name, he checked it by moving his thumb nail down in the sheet. The fifteenth name was that of P. J. Mitchell, and the address given at the side of the name was thirteen twenty-two West Sixty-ninth Street.

Mason folded the letter abruptly, and thrust it in his pocket.

"Get me Paul Drake on the phone again," he said, and walked into his inner office and slammed the door shut behind him.

When Paul Drake came on the line, he said, "Listen Paul, I want you to do something for me."

"Again?" asked Drake.

"Yes," said Mason. "You haven't got started yet."

"All right, shoot," said the detective.

"Listen," Mason said, slowly, "I want you to get in a car and go out to thirteen twenty-two West Sixty-ninth Street, and get Pete Mitchell out of bed. Now, you've got to handle this carefully so that you don't get yourself in a jam, and me too. You've got to do it along the line of a boob detective who talks too much. Don't ask Mitchell any questions until you give him all the information, see? Tell him that you're a detective, and that George Belter was murdered in his house tonight, and that you understand the number of the gun that did the job was the same number that was on a gun which was sold to this chap, Mitchell. Tell him that you suppose he still has the gun and that there's some mistake in the numbers, but that you'd like to know whether or not he can account for his whereabouts at about midnight or a little later. Ask him if he has the gun, or if he remembers what he did with it. But be sure that you tell him everything before you ask him the questions."

"Just be a big, dumb boob, eh?" asked Drake.

"Be a big, dumb boob," Mason told him, "and cultivate a very short memory afterwards."

"I gotcha," said Drake. "I've got to handle this thing in such a way that I'm in the clear, eh?"

Mason said, wearily, "You handle it just the way I told you, just exactly that way."

Mason slipped the phone back on the receiver. He heard the click of the doorknob, and looked up.

Della Street slipped into the office. Her face was white, and her eyes wide. She pushed the door shut behind her, and walked over to the desk.

"There's a man out in the office that says he knows you," she said. "His name is Drumm, and he's a detective from Police Headquarters."

The door pushed open behind her, and Sidney Drumm

104

thrust a grinning face in the door. His washed-out eyes seemed utterly devoid of life, and he looked more than ever like a clerk who had just climbed down from a high stool, and was puttering about, searching for vouchers.

"Pardon the intrusion," he said, "but I wanted to talk with you before you had time to think up a good one."

Mason smiled. "We get used to poor manners from policemen," he said.

"I'm not a cop," protested Drumm. "I'm just a dick. The cops hate me. I'm a poor, underpaid dick."

"Come in and sit down," Mason invited.

"Wonderful office hours you guys keep," Drumm remarked. "I was looking all over for you, and saw a light up here in the office."

"No, you didn't," Mason corrected him, "I've got the shades drawn."

"Oh, well," Drumm said, still grinning, "I had a hunch you were here anyway, because I know you're such a hard worker."

Mason said, "All right. Never mind the kidding. I presume this is a professional call."

"Sure it is," said Drumm, "I've got curiosity. I'm a bird that makes a living by having curiosity and getting it gratified. Right now I'm curious about that telephone number. You come to me and slip me a bit of change in order to strong-arm a private number out of the telephone company. I bust out and get the number for you, and an address, and you thank me for it very politely. Then you show up at that address, sitting around with a murdered guy and a woman. The question is, is it a coincidence?"

"What's the answer?" asked Mason.

"No," said Drumm, "I can't speculate. I asked the question. *You* have to give me the answer."

"The answer," Mason told him, "is that I was out there at the request of the wife."

"Funny you'd know the man's wife, and wouldn't know the man," insisted Drumm.

"Isn't it?" said Mason sarcastically. "Of course that's the worst part of running a law office. So many times a woman will come in and ask you about something, particularly if it happens to be a domestic problem, and won't bring her husband along so that you can see what he looks like. In fact, I've even heard of two or three instances where women went to law offices and didn't want their husbands to know anything about it. But of course that's just a rumor and hearsay, and I wouldn't want you to take my word for it."

Drumm kept grinning. "Well," he said, "would you say that this was *that* kind of a case?"

"I would say nothing," Mason replied.

Drumm quit grinning, and tilted his head back, his eyes became dreamy as they looked at the ceiling.

"That gives it an interesting angle," he said. "Wife comes to attorney who is noted for his ability to get people out of trouble. Attorney doesn't know husband's private telephone number. Attorney starts working on case for wife. Attorney uncovers telephone number. Attorney traces telephone number to husband, and goes out there. Wife there, husband murdered."

Mason's voice was impatient. "Do you think you're getting anywhere, Sidney?"

Drumm grinned once more. "I'll be damned if I know, Perry," he said. "But I'm moving around."

"Let me know as soon as you get anywhere, will you?" asked Mason.

Drumm got to his feet. "Oh," he said, "you'll know it fast enough." He grinned from Mason to Della Street.

"I presume," he said, "that last remark of yours was my cue to get out."

"Oh, don't be in any hurry," Mason told him. "You know we come down to the office at three and four o'clock in the morning just to be here to receive friends who want to ask us foolish questions. We don't really have any work to do. It's just a habit we've gotten into, of getting down here early."

Drumm paused to stare at the lawyer. "You know, Perry, if you'd come clean with me, I might be able to help you a little bit. But if you're going to stand off and be snooty, I've got to go out and pry around a little bit."

"Sure," Mason admitted, "I understand that. That's your business. You've got your profession, and I've got mine."

"That means, I take it," said Drumm, "that you're going to be snooty."

"That means," said Mason, "that you've got to find out your facts on the outside."

"So long, Perry."

"So long, Sidney. Drop in again some time."

"Don't worry, I will."

Sidney Drumm closed the door behind him.

The girl moved impulsively toward Perry Mason.

He waved her back with a motion of his hand, and said, "Take a look in that outer office and make sure he's gone."

She moved toward the door, but, before her hand touched the knob, it turned, and flung open. Sidney Drumm thrust his head into the room again.

He surveyed them and grinned.

"Well," he said, "you didn't fall for that one. All right, Perry, *this* time I'll go out."

"Okay," said Perry Mason. "Good-by!"

Drumm closed the door, and a moment later slammed the door of the outer office.

It was then about four o'clock in the morning.

11

PERRY MASON PULLED HIS HAT DOWN ON HIS HEAD AND
slipped into his overcoat which was still damp enough
to give forth a smell of wet wool.

"I'm going out and chase down a few clews," he told
Della Street. "Sooner or later they're going to start nar-
rowing the circle, and then I won't be able to move. I've
got to do everything while I can still move around. You
stick right here and hold the fort. I can't leave word
where you can reach me, because I'm afraid to have you
call me. But I'll call you every once in a while and ask if
Mr. Mason is in. I'll tell you my name is Johnson, that
I'm an old friend of his, and ask if he left any message.
You can manage to let me know what's going on without letting on who I am."

"You think that they'll have the telephone line
tapped?"

"They may. I don't know just where this thing is going
to lead."

"And they'll have a warrant out for you?"

"Not a warrant, but they'll want to ask me some
more questions."

She looked at him sympathetically, tenderly, said nothing.

"Be careful," he said, and walked out of the office.

It was still dark when he entered the lobby of the
Hotel Ripley, and asked for a room with bath. He reg-

istered under the name of Fred B. Johnson, of Detroit, and was given room 518, for which he was required to pay in advance, inasmuch as he had no baggage.

He went to the room, pulled the curtains, ordered four bottles of ginger ale, with plenty of ice, and got a quart of whiskey from the bellboy. Then he sat in the overstuffed chair, with his feet on the bed, and smoked.

The door was unlocked.

He was smoking for more than half an hour, lighting one cigarette from the tip of the other, when the door opened. Eva Belter came in without knocking.

She closed the door behind her, locked it, and smiled at him. "Oh, I'm so glad that you were here all right."

Perry Mason kept his seat. "You're sure you weren't followed?" he asked.

"No, they didn't follow me. They told me that I was going to be a material witness and that I mustn't leave town, or do anything without communicating with the police. Tell me, do you think they'll arrest me?"

"That depends," he said.

"Depends on what?"

"Depends on lots of things. I want to talk with you."

"All right," she said. "I found the will."

"Where did you find it?"

"In his desk."

"What did you do with it?"

"Brought it with me."

"Let's see it."

"It's just like I thought it was," she said, "only I didn't come off as well as I had expected. I thought that he would at least leave me enough to let me go to Europe and look around, and . . . and sort of get readjusted."

"You mean and get yourself another man."

"I didn't say any such thing!"

"I didn't talk about what you *said*. I was talking about what you *meant*," Mason told her, still using that calmly detached tone of voice.

109

Her face became dignified.

"Really, Mr. Mason," she said, "I think the conversation is wandering rather far afield. Here is the will."

He stared thoughtfully at her. "If you're going to drag me into murder cases," he said, "you'd better not try those upstage tactics. They don't work."

She drew herself up haughtily, then suddenly laughed. "Of course I meant I wanted to get another husband," she said. "Why shouldn't I?"

"All right. Why did you deny it then?"

"I don't know. I couldn't help it. It's just something in me that resents having people know too much about me."

"You mean," he told her, "that you hate the truth. You'd rather build up a protective barrier of falsehoods."

She flushed.

"That's not fair!" she blazed.

He stretched out his hand, without answering her, and took the paper from her hand. He read it slowly.

"All in his handwriting?" he asked.

"No," she said, "I don't think it is."

He looked at her closely.

"It *seems* to be all in the same handwriting."

"I don't think it's his writing."

He laughed. "That won't get you any place," he said. "Your husband showed the will to Carl Griffin and Arthur Atwood, Griffin's attorney, and told them that it was his will and in his handwriting."

The woman shook her head impatiently. "You mean that he showed them *a* will, and said it was in his handwriting. There was nothing to prevent Griffin from tearing up that will, and substituting a forged one. Was there?"

He looked at her in cold appraisal.

"Listen," he said, "you're saying lots of words. Do you know what they mean?"

"Of course, I know what they mean."

"Well," he told her, "that's a dangerous accusation to make, unless you've got something to back it up with."

"I haven't got anything to back it up with—yet," she said, slowly.

"All right, then," he warned, "don't make the accusation."

Her voice was edged with impatience. "You keep telling me that you're my lawyer, and I'm to tell you everything. And then when I tell you everything, you start scolding me."

"Oh, forget it," he said, and handed her back the will. "You can save that injured innocence until you get into court. Now tell me about this will. How did you get it?"

"It was in his study," she said, slowly. "The safe was unlocked. I sneaked out the will and then locked the safe."

"You know that isn't even funny," he told her.

"You don't believe me?"

"Of course not."

"Why?"

"Because the police would probably keep a guard in the room. In any event they would have noticed if the safe had been open and inventoried the contents."

She lowered her eyes, then said slowly, "Do you remember when we went back there? You were looking at the dead body, feeling the bathrobe?"

"Yes," he said, his eyes narrowed.

"All right. I slipped it out of the safe then. The safe was open. I locked it. You were examining the body."

He blinked. "By God," he said, "I believe you did! You *were* over there near the desk and the safe. Why did you do it? Why didn't you tell me what you were up to?"

"Because I wanted to see if the will was in my favor, or whether I could destroy it. Do you think I should destroy it?"

His answer was an explosive, "No!"

She remained silent for several minutes.

"Well," she asked at length, "is there anything else?"

"Yes," he said, "sit down over there on the bed where I can look at you. Now I want to know some things. I

111

didn't ask them before the officers had talked with you because I was afraid I'd get you all rattled. I wanted you to have all the poise you could have when you were talking with them. But now the situation is different. I want to know *exactly* what happened."

She widened her eyes, let her face take on that look of synthetic innocence she affected and said: "I told you what happned."

He shook his head. "No, you didn't."

"Are you accusing me of lying?"

He sighed. "For God's sake, forget that stuff and get down to earth."

"Exactly what is it you want to know?"

"You had on your glad rags last night," he said.

"What do you mean?"

"You know what I mean. You were all dolled up in your evening gown, without any back, and with your satin shoes, and Sunday-go-to-meeting stockings."

"Well?"

"And your husband had been taking a bath."

"Well, what of that?"

"You didn't dress up just on your husband's account," he said.

"Of course not."

"Do you dress every evening?"

"Sometimes."

"As a matter of fact," he said, "you were out last night, and didn't get back in until shortly before your husband was murdered. Isn't that right?"

She shook her head vigorously. Once more her manner became frigidly dignified.

"No," she said, "I was in all evening."

Perry Mason looked at her with cold, searching eyes.

"The housekeeper told me when I was down in the kitchen getting some coffee that she heard your maid tell you that somebody had rung up with a message about some shoes," he ventured.

112

It was obvious that Eva Belter was taken by surprise but she controlled herself with an effort.

"Why, what's wrong with that?" she asked.

"Tell me first," said Mason, "whether or not your maid did bring you such a message."

"Why, yes," said Eva Belter, casually, "I think she did. I can't be certain. I had some shoes that I was very anxious to get, and there has been some trouble about them. I think that Marie received some message about them, and told me what it was. The events crowded it out of my mind."

"Do you know anything at all about how they hang people?" Perry Mason asked abruptly.

"What do you mean?" she demanded.

"For murder," he went on. "It usually happens along in the morning. They come down to the death cell and read the death warrant. Then they strap your hands behind your back, and strap a board along your back, so that you can't cave in. They start a march down the corridor to the scaffold. There are thirteen steps that you have to climb, and then you walk over and stand on a trap. There are prison officials standing by the side of the trap, who look things over, and, in a little cubby-hole back of the trap, are three convicts with sharp knives. There are three strings that run across a board. The hangman puts a noose over your head, and a black bag, and then puts straps around your legs . . ."

She screamed.

"All right. That's exactly what's coming to you if you don't tell me the God's truth."

Her face was white, her lips pale and quivering, and her eyes dark with panic.

"I'm t-t-t-telling you the truth," she said.

He shook his head. "Listen," he told her, "you've got to learn to be frank and to come clean if we're going to get you out of this jam. Now you know, and I know, that that message about the shoes was just a stall. It was a code that you had, meaning that Harrison Burke wanted you to get in touch with him. Just the same way you gave me a code to tell the maid when I wanted to get in touch with you."

She was still shaken and white. Dumbly she nodded her head.

"All right," said Mason, "now tell me what happened. Harrison Burke sent that message to you. He wanted you to get in touch with him. Then you told him that you would meet him some place, and you put on your things and went out. Is that right?"

"No," she said, "he came to the house."

"He did *what?*"

"It's a fact," she went on. "I told him not to, but he came anyway. He wanted to talk with me, and I told him that I wouldn't, that I couldn't see him. So he came to the house. You had told him that George was the owner of *Spicy Bits*. At first he wouldn't believe it. Finally he did. Then he wanted to talk with George. He thought that he could explain to George. He was willing to do anything in order to keep *Spicy Bits* from going ahead with its attack."

"You didn't know he was coming?" he asked.

"No."

There was a moment's silence.

Then she said, "How did you know?"

"Know what?"

"About the shoes being the code he used."

"Oh, he told me," said Mason.

"And then the housekeeper told you about the message?" she asked. "I wonder if she told the police."

Mason shook his head, and smiled.

"No," he said, "she didn't tell the police and she didn't tell me. That was just a little bluff I resorted to in order to get you to give me the real facts. I knew that you must have seen Harrison Burke some time last night, and I knew that he was the kind that would be trying to get in touch with you. When he's worried, he wants some one to share his worry with him. So I figured that he must have left that message with the maid."

She looked hurt.

"Do you think that's a nice way to treat me?" she asked. "Do you think that's being fair with me?"

He grinned.

"What a sweet angel *you* are to sit around and talk to a man about playing fair."

She pouted. "I don't like that," she said.

"I didn't think you would," he told her. "There's going to be lots about this you don't like before we get done. So Harrison Burke came to the house, did he?"

"Yes," she said in a weak voice.

"All right, what happened?"

"He kept insisting that he wanted to see George. I told him that it would be suicidal even to go near George. He said that he wouldn't mention my name at all. He thought that if he could go to George and explain the circumstances to him, and tell him that he was willing to do anything after he was elected, George would order Frank Locke to lay off the publicity."

"All right," said Mason, "now we *are* getting someplace. He wanted to go see your husband, and you tried to keep him from doing it. Is that it?"

"Yes."

"Why," he asked, "did you want to keep him from doing it?"

She said slowly, "I was afraid that he would mention my name."

"Did he?" asked Mason.

"I don't know," she said, and then suddenly added: "That is, of course not, he didn't see George at all. He talked with me, and I convinced him that he mustn't talk with George. And then he left the house."

Perry Mason chuckled. "You thought of that trap just

a little bit too late, young lady. So you don't know whether or not he mentioned your name to George, eh?"

She said sullenly: "I told you he didn't see him."

"Yes," he said, "I know, but the fact is that he *did* see him. He went upstairs to his study and talked with him."

"How do you know?"

"Because," he said, "I've got a theory about this thing, and I want to run it down. I've got a pretty good idea of what happened."

"What did happen?" she asked.

He grinned at her.

"*You* know what happened," he told her.

"No, no," she said, "what was it that happened?"

His voice was a steady, expressionless monotone. "So Harrison Burke went upstairs and talked with your husband," he droned. "How long was he up there?"

"I don't know. Not over fifteen minutes."

"That's better. And you didn't see him after he came down?"

"No."

"Now, as a matter of fact," he inquired, "was there a shot fired while Harrison Burke was up there, and *then* did he run down the stairs, and out of the house without saying anything to you?"

She shook her head emphatically. "No," she said, "Burke left before my husband was shot."

"How long before?"

"I don't know, perhaps fifteen minutes. Perhaps longer. Perhaps not quite so long."

"And now," he pointed out, "Harrison Burke can't be found."

"What do you mean?"

"Exactly what I said. He can't be found. He doesn't answer his telephone. He isn't at his residence."

"How do you know?"

"I kept trying to get him on the telephone, and I sent detectives out to his residence."

116

"Why did you do that?"

"Because I knew he was going to be implicated in the shooting."

She widened her eyes again. "How could that be?" she asked. "Nobody knows that he was out at the house except us. And of course we wouldn't tell, because that would make the situation that much worse for everybody. He left before the other man came, who fired the shot."

Perry Mason held her eyes in a steady gaze. "It was his gun that fired the shot," he said, slowly.

She stared at him, her eyes startled.

"What makes you say that?" she asked.

"Because," he told her, "there was a number on the gun. That number can be traced from the factory to the wholesaler, from the wholesaler to the retailer, and from the retailer to the man who bought the gun. It was a fellow named Pete Mitchell, who lives at thirteen twenty-two West Sixty-ninth Street, and was a close friend of Harrison Burke's. The police are rounding up Mitchell, and when they get him, he'll have to explain what he did with the gun. That is, that he gave it to Burke."

She put a hand to her throat.

"How can they trace guns like that?"

"There's a record kept of everything."

"I knew that we should have done something with that gun," she said almost hysterically.

He said, "Yes, and then you *would* have put your head in the noose. You've got yourself to think of. Your own position in this is none too pretty. You want to save Burke, of course, if you can. But the thing that I'm trying to bring out is, that *if* Burke did the thing, you'd better come clean and tell me. Then, if we can keep Burke out of it, we will. But I don't want you to get in the position where they build up a case against you, while you're trying to shield Burke."

She started to pace the floor, twisting her handkerchief in her fingers.

"Oh, my God!" she said. "Oh, my God! Oh, my God!"

"I don't know whether or not it's ever occurred to you," he said, "but there's a penalty for being an accessory after the fact, or for compounding a felony. Now, we don't either one of us want to get in that position. What we want to do is to find out who did this thing, and find it out before the police do. I don't want them to frame a murder charge on you, and I don't want them to frame one on me. If Burke is guilty, the thing to do is to get in touch with Burke, and get him to surrender himself, and rush the case through to a trial before the District Attorney's office can get too much evidence. I'm going to take steps to see that Locke keeps quiet, and call off this blackmail article in *Spicy Bits*."

She stared at him for a moment, and then asked, "How are you going to do that?"

He smiled at her. "In this game," he said, "I'm the one that has to know everything. The less you know, the less you stand a chance of telling."

"You can trust me. I can keep a secret," she told him.

"You're a good liar," he said judiciously, "if that's what you mean. But this is once where you won't have to lie, because you won't know what's going on."

"But Burke didn't do it," she insisted.

He frowned at her.

"Now listen," he said, "that's the reason I wanted to get in touch with you. If Burke didn't do it, *who did?*"

She shifted her eyes. "I told you some man had a conference with my husband. I don't know who he was. I thought it was you. It sounded like your voice."

He got to his feet, and his face darkened.

"Listen," he said, "if you go trying that kind of a game on me, I'll throw you to the wolves. You've tried that game once. That's enough."

She started to cry and sobbed. "I c-c-can't help it. You asked me. There's nobody listening. I t-t-told you who it

118

w-w-was. I heard your v-v-voice. I won't t-t-tell the p-p-police, not even if they t-t-torture me!"

He took her by the shoulders and slammed her down on the bed. He pulled her hands from her face and stared at her eyes. There was no trace of tears in them.

"Now listen," he said, "you *didn't* hear my voice, because I wasn't there at all. And cut out that sobbing act—unless you've got an onion in your handkerchief!"

"Then it was somebody whose voice sounded like yours," she insisted.

He scowled at her.

"Are you in love with Burke?" he asked. "And trying to put me in a position where you can throw me over in case I can't square the thing for Burke?"

"No. You wanted me to tell the truth, and I'm telling it."

"I'm tempted to get up and walk out on you, and leave you with the whole mess on your hands," he threatened.

She said, demurely, "Then, of course, I'd *have* to tell the police whose voice it was I heard in that room."

"So *that's* your little game, eh?"

"I haven't any game. I'm telling the truth." Her voice was sweet, but she didn't meet his eyes.

Mason sighed. "I never went back on a client yet, guilty or innocent," he said. "I'm trying to remember that. But, by God! It's a temptation to walk out on *you!*"

She sat on the bed and twisted her handkerchief about her fingers.

In a moment he began to talk, "On my way back down the hill, after I'd left your house, I stopped to talk with the clerk in the drug store where you telephoned to me. He was watching you when you went in the telephone booth, which was only natural. A woman in evening clothes, with a man's coat on, who is sopping wet, and goes into a telephone booth, in an all night drug store, after midnight, is naturally going to attract some attention.

119

Now this clerk told me that you called *two* telephone numbers."

Wide-eyed she looked at him, but she said nothing.

"Who did you call besides me?" he asked.

"Nobody," she said, "the clerk's mistaken."

Perry Mason put on his hat and pulled it low down over his forehead. He turned to Eva Belter and said savagely, "I'm going to get you out of this somehow. I don't know just how. But I'm going to get you out of it. And, by God, it's going to cost you money!"

He jerked open the door, went out into the hall, and slammed the door behind him. The first light of dawn was coloring the eastern sky.

12

■

THE FIRST RAYS OF THE EARLY MORNING SUN WERE gilding the tops of the buildings, when Perry Mason got hold of Harrison Burke's housekeeper.

She was fifty-seven or eight years old, heavily fleshed, filled with animosity. Her eyes were sparkling with hostility.

"I don't care *who* you are," she said, truculently. "I tell you that he isn't here. I don't know where he is. He was out until around midnight, then he got a telephone call, and went out again. After that, the telephone kept ringing all night. I didn't answer it, because I knew he wasn't here, and my feet get cold when I get up in the middle of the night. And I don't appreciate being called out of bed at this hour, either!"

"How long after he came in before there was a telephone call?" asked Mason.

"It wasn't very long, if it's really any of your business."

"Do you think he was expecting the telephone call?"

"How do I know? He woke me up when he came in. I heard him open the door and close it. I was trying to go to sleep again when I heard the telephone ring, and heard him talk. Then I heard him run up to his bedroom. I thought he was going to bed, but I guess he was putting some things in a suitcase, because this morning the suitcase is gone. I heard him run down the stairs and slam the front door."

Perry Mason said, "Well, I guess that's all, then."

She said, "You bet it's all!" and slammed the door.

Mason got in his car, and stopped at a hotel to call his office.

When he heard Della Street's voice on the line, he said, "Is Mr. Mason there?"

"No, he isn't," she said. "Who's calling"

"This is a friend of his," he told her, "Mr. Fred B. Johnson. I wanted to get in touch with Mr. Mason very badly."

"I can't tell you where he is," she said rapidly, "but I expect he'll be in soon. There are several people looking for him, and one of them, a Mr. Paul Drake, I think has an appointment. So I think he'll be in soon."

"Well, that's all right," Mason remarked, casually. "I'll call again."

"You haven't any message to leave with *me?*" she asked.

"Nothing," he told her, "except that I'll call again," and he hung up.

He called back the number of Drake's Detective Bureau and got Paul Drake on the telephone.

"Don't make any cracks where anybody can hear you, Paul," said Mason, "because I have an idea a lot of people

121

would like to ask me some questions that I'd rather not answer right now. You know who this is."

"Yeah," replied Drake, "I got some funny dope for you."

"Shoot," said Mason.

"I went out to this chap's house. The one on West Sixty-ninth Street, and I found something funny."

"Go on," Mason told him.

"This bird got a telephone call from somebody a little after midnight, and told his wife that he was called out of town on important business. He seemed pretty much frightened. He put some things in a suitcase, and, about quarter to one, an automobile drove by for him, and he got in and left. He told his wife that he'd get in touch with her and let her know where he was. This morning she received a telegram saying: *'All right. Don't worry. Love.'*, and that's all she knows. Naturally she was a bit worried."

"That's fine," Mason said.

"Does it mean anything to you?" asked Drake.

"I think it does," said Mason. "I've got to think it over a bit. I think it means a whole lot. Have you got anything new on Locke?"

Drake's voice showed animation. "I haven't found out what you want to know yet, Perry. But I think I'm on the tracks of it all right. You remember this jane at the Wheelright Hotel? This Esther Linten?"

"Yeah," said Mason. "What about her?"

"Well," said Drake, "it's a funny thing, but she came from Georgia."

Mason whistled.

"That's not all," went on Drake. "She's getting some regular sugar from Locke. There's a check that goes through every two weeks, and it's a check that doesn't come from Locke himself. It comes from a special account that *Spicy Bits* keeps in a downtown bank. We managed to get the cashier at the hotel to talk. The kid has been cashing the checks through the hotel regularly."

"Can you trace her back to Georgia and find out what she's been mixed up in?" Mason asked. "Maybe she hasn't changed her name."

"That's what we're working on now," Drake said. "I've got the Georgia agency working on it. I told them to send me a wire just as soon as they had anything that looked definite, and not to wait until they had run it down, but to keep reporting progress."

"That's fine," Mason said. "Can you tell me where Frank Locke was last night?"

"Every minute of the time. We had a shadow on that boy that stuck to him all evening. Do you want a complete report?"

"Yes," said Mason. "Right away."

"Where shall I send it?"

"Make sure that your messenger isn't followed, and is somebody you can trust. Have him drop in at the Hotel Ripley, and leave it at the desk for Fred B. Johnson of Detroit."

"Fine," said Drake. "Keep in touch with me. I may want to get you."

"Okay," agreed Mason, and hung up.

He went at once to the Hotel Ripley, and asked at the desk if there was anything for Mr. Johnson. Upon being advised that there was not, he went up to 518 and tried the door. It was unlocked. He walked in.

Eva Belter sat on the edge of the bed, smoking. There was a highball glass in front of her on the stand by the bed. The whiskey bottle stood beside the glass. It was about a third empty.

In the overstuffed chair sat a big man with wavering eyes, who looked uncomfortable.

Eva Belter said, "I'm glad you came. You wouldn't believe me, so I brought you some proof."

"Proof of what?" asked Mason. He was staring at the big man who had risen from the overstuffed chair, and was regarding Mason from embarrassed eyes.

123

"Proof of the fact that the will's a forgery," she said. "This is Mr. Dagett. He's the cashier at the bank where George handled all of his business. He knows a good deal about George's private affairs. He says it's not his writing."

Dagett bowed and smiled. "You're Mr. Mason," he said, "the attorney? I'm glad to meet you."

He did not offer to shake hands.

Mason planted his feet wide apart, and looked into the uncomfortable eyes of the big man.

"Never mind squirming around," he said. "She's got some hold on you or you wouldn't be here at this hour of the morning. Probably you ring up the maid and leave a message about a hat or something. I don't give a damn about that. What I want now are the straight facts. Never mind what she *wants* you to say. I'm telling you you're giving her the most help by being on the square. Is this thing on the level?"

The banker's face changed color. He took a half stride toward the lawyer, then stopped, took a deep breath, and said: "You mean about the will?"

"About the will," said the lawyer.

"It is," said Dagett. "I've examined that will carefully. It's a forgery. And the remarkable thing about it is that it's not a very good forgery at that. If you'll study it closely, you can see that the character of the handwriting broke down once or twice in it. It's as though some one tried to make a hasty forgery, and became fatigued during the process."

Mason snapped, "Let me see that will."

Eva Belter passed it over.

"How about another highball, Charlie?" she asked the banker, and tittered.

Dagett shook his head, savagely. "No," he said, vehemently.

Mason examined the will carefully. His eyes narrowed. "By God!" he said. "You're right!"

"There can be no question of it," Dagett told him.

124

Mason turned to him sharply, "You're willing to go on the stand and testify?" he asked.

"Good heavens, no! But you don't need me! It's self-evident."

Perry Mason stared at him. "All right," he said. "That's all."

Dagett walked to the door, flung it open and hurried out of the room.

Mason fastened his eyes on Eva Belter.

"Listen," he said, "I told you you could meet me here to talk things over, but I didn't want you to stick around the room. Don't you realize what a position we'd be in if they discovered us here in one room at this hour of the morning?"

She shrugged her shoulders.

"We've got to take *some* risks," she said, "and I wanted you to talk with Mr. Dagett."

"How did you get him?" he asked.

"Called him on the telephone and told him to come over, it was important. And it wasn't nice of you to say the things you did to him. It was naughty!"

She giggled with alcoholic mirth.

"You know him pretty well?" asked Mason.

"What do you mean?" she asked.

He stood staring at her. "You know damned well what I mean. You called him Charlie."

"Certainly," she said. "That's his first name. He's a friend of mine, as well as George's."

"I see," said Mason.

He went to the telephone and called his office.

"Mr. Johnson," he said. "Has Mr. Mason come in yet?"

"No," said Della Street, "he hasn't. I'm afraid he's going to be awfully busy when he does come in, Mr. Johnson. Something happened last night. I don't know exactly what it was, but it was a murder case of some kind, and Mr. Mason is representing one of the main witnesses. There have been some newspaper reporters trying to see him, and there's some one who insists on staying in the outer office. I think he's a police detective. So I'm very much afraid that if you were counting on seeing Mr. Mason at the office this morning, you're going to be disappointed."

"Gee, that's too bad," Mason said. "I have some papers to dictate that I know Mr. Mason would want to see, and probably he'd have to sign them. I wonder if you could tell me some one who could take them down in shorthand?"

"I think I could," said Della Street.

"I was just wondering," said Mason, "whether *you* could get away with all of the people that are around there."

"Leave it to me," she said.

"I'm at the Hotel Ripley," he told her.

"Okay," she said, and hung up.

Mason stared at Eva Belter moodily.

"All right," he said, "since you're here, and you've risked this much, you're going to stay here for a while."

"What's going to happen?"

"I'm going to file a petition for letters of administration," he said. "That will force them to come out and offer the will for probate, and then we're going to file a contest to the probate of the will, and make an application to have you appointed a special administratrix."

"What does all that mean?"

"That means," he told her, "that you're going to be in the saddle from now on, and we're going to keep you there no matter what they do."

"What good will that do?" she asked. "If I'm virtually disinherited under the will, we've got to *prove* it's a forgery, and I can't get anything until after there's been a trial and a judgment. Can I?"

"I'm thinking about the management of the properties of the estate," said Mason, *"Spicy Bits* for instance."

"Oh," she said, "I see."

126

Mason went on, "We're going to dictate these papers all at once, and leave them with my secretary so that she can file them, one at a time. You've got to take that will and put it back. They'll probably have a guard in the room so you can't return it where you found it, but you can plant it some place in the house."

She tittered once more. "I can do that, too," she said.

Mason said: "You do take the damnedest chances. Why you fished that will out of there is more than I know. If you're caught with it, it might be serious."

"Cheer up," she told him, "I won't be caught with it. *You* don't ever take a chance, do you?"

"My God!" he said. "I took a chance when I started in mixing in your business. You're plain dynamite."

She smiled seductively at him. "Do you think so?" she said. "I know some men who like women that way."

He stared moodily at her.

"You're getting drunk," he told her. "Lay off that whiskey."

"My," she said, "you talk just like a husband."

He walked over, picked up the whiskey bottle, jammed the cork in, put the bottle in the drawer of the bureau, locked the drawer and put the key in his pocket.

"Was that nice?" she asked.

"Yes," he said.

The telephone rang. Mason answered it. The clerk advised him that a messenger had just arrived with a package for him.

Mason said to have a boy bring the package up, and hung up.

When the bellboy knocked at the door, Mason was standing at the knob. He opened the door, handed the boy a tip, and took the envelope. It was the report from the Detective Agency concerning the activities of Frank Locke on the preceding evening.

"What is it?" asked Eva Belter.

He shook his head, walked over to the window, opened the envelope, and started reading the typewritten report.

It was rather simple. Locke had gone to a speakeasy, stayed there half an hour, gone to a barber shop, had a shave and massage, gone to the Wheelright Hotel, gone to room 946, remained there five or ten minutes, and then had gone to dinner with Esther Linten, the tenant of the room.

They had dined and danced until eleven o'clock, and then had gone back to the room in the Wheelright. Bell-boys had brought up ginger ale and ice, and Locke had stayed in the room until one-thirty in the morning, when he had left.

Mason thrust the reports into his pocket and started drumming with the tips of his fingers on the sash of the window.

"You make me nervous," said Eva Belter. "I wish you'd tell me what's going on."

"I've told you what we're going to do."

"What were those papers?"

"A business matter."

"What business?"

He laughed at her. "Do I have to tell you the business of *all* of my clients just because I happen to be working for you?"

She frowned at him. "I think you're horrid."

He shrugged his shoulders and continued drumming upon the sash of the window.

There was a knock at the door.

"Come in," he called.

The door opened and Della Street walked in. She stiffened as she saw Eva Belter on the bed.

"Okay, Della," said Mason. "We've got to have some papers ready for an emergency that may arise. We've got to figure on a petition for letters of administration, on a contest for the probate of a will, and on an application for special letters of administration, an order appointing Mrs.

Belter as special administratrix, and a bond all ready to submit for approval and filing. Then we've got to have special letters of administration, with copies to be certified and served on interested parties."

Della Street asked coolly, "Do you wish to dictate them now?"

"Yes, and I want some breakfast."

He went to the telephone, rang room service, and ordered breakfast sent up.

Della Street stared at Eva Belter. "I'm sorry," she said, "but I'll have to have that table."

Eva Belter arched her eyebrows and picked up her glass from the table, much with the gesture of a woman gathering her skirts about her when encountering a beggar on the street.

Mason lifted off the ginger ale bottle and the bowl of ice, polished the top of the table with the moist cover which had been on it, and set it down in front of a chair for Della Street.

She pulled up the straight-back chair, crossed her knees, put the notebook on the table, and poised her pencil.

Perry Mason dictated rapidly for twenty minutes. At the end of that time breakfast arrived. The three ate heartily and almost in silence. Eva Belter managed to give the impression that she was eating with the servants.

When the breakfast was finished, Mason had the things taken away, and proceeded with his dictation. By nine-thirty he had finished.

"Go back to the office and write those up," he told Della, "and have them all ready for signature. But don't let anybody see what you're doing. You'd better keep the outer office door locked. You can use the printed forms for the petitions."

"Okay," she said. "I'd like to see you for a moment alone."

Eva Belter sniffed.

"Don't mind her," said Mason, "she's going."

"Oh, no, I'm not," Eva Belter said.

"Yes, you are," Mason ordered. "You're going right now. I had to have you here while I was dictating those papers in order to get the information that I needed. You're going back and put that will back in the house. Then you're going up to my office this afternoon and sign all of these papers. And, in the meantime, you're going to keep your own counsel. The newspaper reporters are going to ask you questions. They'll get in touch with you somewhere along the line. You're going to use all of your sex appeal and be shocked and crushed by the terrible misfortune you've suffered. You're going to be unable to give out any kind of a coherent interview, and you're going to sell them on your grief. Every time they stick a camera your way, show lots of leg and turn on the water works. Do you understand?"

"You're coarse," she said coldly.

"I'm effective," he told her. "What the hell's the use of you trying to slip a lot of stuff over on me when you know it doesn't go?"

She put on her hat and coat with dignity and marched to the door.

"Just when I get so I really like you," she told him, "you have to go ahead and spoil it all."

He silently held the door open for her, bowed her out and then slammed it shut.

He moved over close to Della Street, and said, "What is it, Della?"

She reached down the front of her dress and pulled out an envelope.

"A messenger brought this."

"What is it?" he asked.

"Money."

He opened the flap of the envelope. There were one hundred dollar traveler checks on the inside. Two books with one thousand dollars in each book. All of the checks

130

were signed "Harrison Burke" and duly counter-signed. The name of the payee was left blank.

There was a note attached to the checks, scribbled hurriedly in pencil.

Mason unfolded the note, and read it: "I THOUGHT IT WOULD BE BETTER FOR ME TO KEEP OUT OF THE WAY FOR A LITTLE WHILE. GO AHEAD AND KEEP ME OUT OF THIS. NO MATTER WHAT HAPPENS, *keep me out of it.*" The note was signed with the initials "H.B."

Mason handed the books over to Della Street.

"Business," he said, "is looking up. Be careful where you cash them."

She nodded her head.

"Tell me, what's happened? What has she got you into?"

"She hasn't got me into anything except a couple of good fees. And before she gets done, she's going to pay more."

"She has too," insisted Della. "She's got you mixed up in that murder case. I heard some of the reporters talking this morning. She got you out there before she notified the police, and she's framed things so that she can drag you into it at any time. What makes you think she isn't going to tell the police you were the man who was in the room when the shot was fired?"

Mason made a weary gesture.

"I don't," he said. "I have an idea that she's going to do that sooner or later."

"Are you going to stand for it?"

The lawyer explained patiently.

"When you're representing clients, Della," he said, "you can't pick and choose them. You've got to take them as they come. There's only one rule in this game, and that is that when you do take them, you've got to give them all you've got."

She sniffed. "That doesn't mean that you have to sit

131

back and let them accuse you of murder in order to protect a sweetheart."

"You're getting pretty wise," Mason remarked. "Who've you been talking to?"

"One of the reporters. Only I haven't been talking. I've been listening."

He smiled at her. "Skip along and get these things out, and don't worry about me. I've got work to do. Whenever you come over here, be careful that nobody shadows you."

"This is the last time I dare to try it," she said. "I had an awful time getting away. They tried to follow me. I pulled the same stunt that Mrs. Belter did the first time she came to the office, of going through the dressing-room. It always bothers a man when he's trailing a woman, and she walks into a ladies' room. They'll fall for it once, but not twice."

"Okay," said Mason. "I've kept under cover almost as long as I can myself. They'll be picking me up sometime today."

"I *hate* her!" Della Street said fervently. "I wish you'd never seen her. She isn't worth the money. If we made ten times as much money out of it, she still wouldn't be worth it. I told you just what she was—all velvet and claws!"

"Wait a minute, young lady," Mason warned. "You haven't seen the blow-off yet."

Della Street tossed her head. "I've seen enough. I'll have these things all ready by this afternoon."

"Okay," said Mason. "Let her sign them, and see that everything's in order. I may have to grab them and run, or telephone you and have you meet me some place."

She flashed him a smile and went out, very trim, very self-possessed, loyal and very worried.

Mason waited five minutes, and then lit a cigarette, and walked out of the hotel.

132

13

Mason paused at the door of room 946 in the Wheelright Hotel and tapped gently on the panels. There was no sound from within. He waited a moment, then knocked a little more loudly.

After a few moments, he heard a stir from the interior of the room, the creak of bed springs, and then a woman's voice saying, "Who is it?"

"Telegram," said Perry Mason.

He heard the door latch click on the inside, and the door open. Mason lowered his shoulder, pushed the door back and walked into the room.

The girl had on pajamas of the sheerest silk which revealed the details of her figure. She had been sleeping, and her eyes were swollen. Her face still had traces of make-up but showed a certain sallow color of skin beneath the cosmetics.

Seeing her in the light of the morning, Mason knew that she was older than he had at first thought. She was, however, beautiful, and her figure would have been the delight of a sculptor. Her eyes were large and dark. There was a sullen pout to the mouth.

She stood before him without any semblance of modesty, but with a certain air of sullen defiance about her.

"What's the idea of busting in here this way?" she asked.

"I wanted to talk with you."

"That's a hell of a way to do it," said the girl.

Mason nodded. "Get back into bed. You'll catch cold."

"Just for that," she said, "I don't think I will."

She crossed to the window, raised the shade, and turned to face him.

"Well," she said, "spill it."

"I'm sorry," said Mason, "but you're in a jam."

"Says you!" she retorted.

"It happens that I'm telling you the truth."

"Who do you think you are?"

"My name's Mason."

"A detective?"

"No, a lawyer."

"Huh."

"I happen to represent Mrs. Eva Belter," he went on. "Does that mean anything to you?"

"Not a damn thing."

"Well," he protested, "don't get hard about it. You might at least be sociable."

She made a grimace, spat forth a swift comment, "I *hate* to have my sleep interrupted at this hour in the morning, and I *hate* men who come busting in the way you did."

Mason ignored her statement. "Did you know that Frank Locke didn't own *Spicy Bits*?" he asked casually.

"Who's Frank Locke, and what's *Spicy Bits*?"

He laughed at her.

"Frank Locke," he said, "is the man who's been signing the checks on the special account of *Spicy Bits*, which you've been cashing every two weeks."

"You're one of these smart guys, ain't you?" she said.

"I get around," Mason admitted.

"Well, what about it?"

"Locke was a figurehead. A man by the name of Belter owned the paper. Locke did what Belter told him to."

She stretched up her arms and yawned. "Well, what's that to me? Have you got a cigarette?"

Mason handed her a cigarette. She came close to him

134

while he applied the match, then strolled over and sat down on the bed, tucked her feet up in under her, and hugged her knees.

"Go on," she said, "if it interests you. I reckon I can't get to sleep until after you leave."

"You're not going to sleep any more today."

"No?"

"No. There's a morning paper outside the door. Would you like to see it?"

"Why?"

"It tells all about the murder of George C. Belter."

"I hate murders before breakfast."

"You might like to read about this one anyway."

"All right," she said, "go get me the paper."

He shook his head at her.

"No," he said, "*you* get the paper. Otherwise, when I open the door something might happen, and I'd get pushed out."

She got up, puffing placidly at the cigarette, crossed to the door, opened it, reached out and picked up the paper.

The headlines screamed the news of the Belter murder. She walked back to the bed, sat down with her feet tucked in under her, legs crossed, and read through the paper, smoking as she read.

"Well," she said. "I still don't see that it's anything in my young life. Some guy got bumped. It's too bad, but he probably had it coming to him."

"He did," said Mason.

"Well, why should that make me lose my beauty sleep?"

"If you'll use your noodle," he explained patiently, "you'll find out that Mrs. Belter has come into a position where she controls all of the property in the estate and I happen to represent Mrs. Belter."

"Well?"

"You've been blackmailing Frank Locke," he said, "and Locke has been embezzling trust funds in order to pay the blackmail. That special account of *Spicy Bits* was an

135

account that was given him to use in purchasing information. He's been handing it over to you."

"I'm in the clear," she said, tossing the paper to the floor, "I didn't know anything at all about it."

He laughed at her.

"How about the blackmail?"

"I don't know what you're talking about."

"Oh, yes, you do, Esther. You are shaking him down on account of this Georgia business."

That remark registered with her. Her face changed color, and, for the first time, there was a startled look in her eyes.

Mason went on to press his advantage.

"That," he said, "wouldn't look pretty. You may have heard of compounding a felony. It's a crime in this state, you know."

She appraised him watchfully. "You're not a dick, just a lawyer?"

"Just a lawyer."

"Okay," she said. "What do you want?"

"*Now* you're commencing to talk turkey."

"I'm not talking; I'm listening."

"You were with Frank Locke last night," he said.

"Who says I was?"

"I do. You went out with him, then came back here, and he stayed until long in the morning."

"I'm free, white, and twenty-one," she said, "and this is my home. I guess I've got a right to entertain men friends if I want to."

"Sure you have," he said. "The next question is, have you got sense enough to know which side of your bread has got the butter?"

"How do you mean?"

"What did you do last night after you got back to the room?"

"Talked about the weather, of course."

"That's fine," he told her. "You had some drinks sent

up, and sat and chatted, and then you got sleepy and went to sleep."

"Who says that?" she asked.

"That's what *I* say," he explained, "and that's what you're *going* to say. You got sleepy and passed out."

Her eyes were thoughtful. "How do you mean?"

Mason spoke as though he had been a teacher coaching a pupil. "You were tired and you'd been drinking. You got into your pajamas and went to sleep about eleven-forty, and you don't know anything that happened after that. You don't know when Frank Locke left."

"What good does it do me if I say I went to sleep?" she inquired.

Mason's tone was casual. "I think Mrs. Belter would be very much inclined to overlook the matter of the embezzled account if you went to sleep as I mentioned."

"Well, I didn't go to sleep."

"You'd better think it over."

She stared at him with her big, appraising eyes and said nothing.

Mason crossed to the telephone and gave the number of Paul Drake's Detective Agency.

"You know who this is, Paul," he said, when he heard Drake's voice. "What have you got, anything?"

"Yes," said Drake, "I've got something on the broad."

"Spill it," said Mason.

"She won a beauty contest in Savannah," said Drake. "She was under age at the time. There was another kid living with her in an apartment. A man got the kid in a jam, and then killed her. He tried to cover up the crime and made a bum job of it. He was arrested and tried. This girl switched her testimony at the last minute and gave him a break. He got a hung jury on the first trial, and managed to escape before they tried him again. He's still a fugitive from justice. His name is Cecil Dawson. I'm looking him up for description and fingerprints, and

137

any more dope I can get. I have an idea that he may be the man you want."

"Okay," Mason said, as though he had expected just that. "That comes in pretty handy right now. Stay with it, and I'll get in touch with you a little later."

He hung up the telephone and turned back to the girl.

"Well," he asked, "what is it, yes or no?"

"No," she said. "I told you that before, and I don't change my mind."

He stared at her, steadily. "You know, the funny part of it is," he said, slowly, "that it goes farther back than just the blackmail. It goes back to the time that you changed your testimony, and gave Dawson an opportunity to get a hung jury. When he's brought back and tried on that murder charge, the fact that you have been here with him and taking these checks from him will put you in kind of a tough spot on a perjury prosecution."

Her face lost its color. Her eyes were big, dark and staring. Her mouth sagged open and she breathed heavily through it.

"My God!" she said.

"Exactly," said Mason. "You were asleep last night."

She kept her eyes on him and asked, "Would that square it?"

"I don't know," Mason told her. "It would square things at this end. I don't know whether anybody's going to make a squawk about the Georgia business or not."

"All right. I was asleep."

Mason got up and moved toward the door.

"You want to remember that," he said. "Nobody knows about this except me. If you tell Locke that I was here, or the proposition I made you, I'll see that you get the works everywhere along the line."

"Don't be silly," she said. "I know when I've had enough."

He walked out and closed the door behind him.

He got in his car and drove to Sol Steinburg's Pawnshop.

Steinburg was fat, with shrewd, twinkling eyes and lips which were twisted in a perpetual smile.

He beamed on Perry Mason, and said, "Well, well, well. It's been a long time since I've seen you, my friend."

Mason shook hands. "It certainly has, Sol. And now I'm in trouble."

The pawnbroker nodded and rubbed his hands together.

"Whenever they get in trouble," he said, "they come to Sol Steinburg's place. What is your trouble, my friend?"

"Listen," said Mason, "I want you to do something for me."

"I'd do anything I could for you, y'understand. Of course, business is business. And if it's a business matter, you've got to come to me on a business basis, and take business treatment. But if it ain't business y'understand, I'd do anything I could."

Mason's eyes twinkled. "It's business for you, Sol," he said, "because you're going to make fifty dollars out of it. But you don't have to invest anything."

The fat man broke out in laughter.

"That," he proclaimed, "is the kind of business I like to talk—when I don't have to invest anything, and make a fifty dollar profit already, I know it's a good business. What do I do?"

"Let me see the register of revolvers you've sold," Mason told him.

The man fished under a counter and produced a well-thumbed booklet, in which had been registered the style and make of the weapon, the number, the person to whom it was sold, and the signature of the purchaser.

Mason thumbed the pages until he found a 32-Colt automatic.

"That's the one," he said.

Steinburg leaned over the book, and stared at the registration.

139

"What about it?"

"I'm coming in here with a man sometime today, or tomorrow," said Mason, "and, as soon as you look at him, you nod your head vigorously, and say, 'That's the man, that's the man, that's the man, all right.' I'll ask you if you're *sure* it's the man and you get more and more certain. He'll deny it, and the more he denies it, the more certain you get!"

Sol Steinburg pursed his thick lips. "That might be serious."

Mason shook his head.

"It would be if you said it in court," he admitted, "but you're not going to say it in court. You're not going to say it to anybody except this man. And you're not going to say what it was he did. Simply identify him as being the man. Then you go in the back part of the store, and leave me with the firearm register here. Do you understand?"

"Sure, sure," said Steinburg. "I understand it fine. All except one thing."

"What's that?" asked Mason.

"Where the fifty dollars is coming from."

Mason slapped his pants pocket. "Right here, Sol." He pulled out a roll of bills from which he took fifty dollars, and handed it to the pawnbroker.

"Anybody you come in with?" he asked. "Is that it?"

"Anybody I come in with," Mason said. "I won't come in here unless I've got the right man. I may have to dress the act up a little bit, but you follow my lead. Is that okay?"

The pawnbroker's caressing fingers folded the fifty dollars.

"My friend," he said, "whatever you do is all right with me. I say whatever I am supposed to say, and I say it loud, y'understand."

"That's fine," said Mason. "Don't get shaken in your identification."

Steinburg put the fifty dollars in his pocket. "I won't," he said, shaking his head vigorously.

Perry Mason walked out, whistling.

14

FRANK LOCKE SAT IN THE EDITORIAL OFFICE AND stared at Perry Mason.

"I understood that they were looking for you," he said.

"Who was?" asked Perry Mason carelessly.

"Reporters, police, detectives. Lots of people," said Locke.

"I saw them all."

"This afternoon?"

"No, last night. Why?"

"Nothing," Locke replied, "except that they may be looking for you in a different way now. What is it you want?"

"I just dropped in to tell you that Eva Belter had filed a petition for letters of administration on her husband's estate."

"What's that to me?" asked Locke, his milk-chocolate eyes on Perry Mason.

"It means that Eva Belter is running things from now on. You're going to take your orders from her," said Mason. "And it means that, inasmuch as I'm representing Eva Belter, you're going to take some orders from me. One of the first things you're going to do is to kill anything about that Beechwood Inn affair."

"Is *that* so?" said Locke, sarcastically.

"That," said Mason, with emphasis, "is so."

"You're what they call an optimist."

"Maybe I am. Again, maybe I'm not. Just take down the telephone and ring up Eva Belter."

"I don't have to ring up Eva Belter, or anybody else. I'm running this newspaper."

"You're going to be like that, are you?"

"Just like that," Locke snapped.

"I might talk with you again if we went some place where I was certain that I could talk without too many people listening," Mason remarked.

"You'd have to make better talk than you did the last time," said Locke, "or I wouldn't be interested in leaving."

"Well, we might take a stroll, Locke, and see if we could come to some terms."

"Why not talk here?"

"You know the way I feel about this place," Mason told him. "It makes me uneasy, and I don't talk well when I'm uneasy."

Locke hesitated for a minute, finally said, "Well, I won't give you over fifteen minutes. You've got to talk turkey this time."

"I can talk turkey," Mason remarked.

"Well, I'm always willing to take a chance," Locke said.

He got his hat and went down to the street with Mason.

"Suppose we get a cab and ride around until we find some place that looks good, where we can talk," said Locke.

"Well, let's walk down the block here, and around the corner. I want to be sure that we get a taxi that isn't planted," Mason said.

Locke made a grimace. "Oh, cut out that kid stuff, Mason! Be your age! I've got the office wired so that I can tune a witness in on the conversation when I want to, but don't think that I've gone to all the trouble of arranging a bunch of stuff on the outside, so I can hear what *you* say. You could have yelled anything you said before

142

from the tops of the skyscrapers, and it wouldn't have made a damned bit of difference."

Mason shook his head.

"No," he said, "when I do business, I do it in just one way."

Locke scowled. "I don't like that way."

"Lots of people don't," Mason admitted.

Locke stood still. "That's not getting you anywhere, Mason. I might as well go back to the office."

"You'll regret it if you do," Mason warned him.

Locked hesitated, and then finally shrugged his shoulders.

"All right," he said, "let's go. I've come this far. I may as well see it through."

Mason walked him down the street until they came to Sol Steinburg's place.

"We'll go in here," said Mason.

Locke flashed him a glance of instant suspicion. "I won't talk in there," he said.

"You don't have to," Mason told him, "we're just going in here, and you can come right out."

"What kind of a frame-up is this?" Locke demanded.

"Oh, come on in," Mason said, impatiently. "Who's getting suspicious now?"

Locke walked on in, looking cautiously about him.

Sol Steinburg came out from the back room with his face wreathed in smiles. He walked up to Mason, and said, "Hello, hello, hello. What do you want today?"

Then he seemed to notice Frank Locke for the first time and stopped smiling. "You back again?" he asked abruptly.

Sol Steinburg's face ran through a gamut of expressions. The smile gave place to an expression of startled recognition. The expression of startled recognition gave way to one of fierce determination. He raised a quivering forefinger, pointed it directly at Locke, and said, "That's the man."

Mason's voice was incisive. "Now, wait a minute, Sol. We've got to be *sure* about this."

The pawnbroker became voluble. "Ain't I sure? Can't I tell a man when I see him? You asked me if I could tell him when I saw him, and I told you, 'yes.' Now I see him, and I tell you yes again. That's him! That's the man! What do you want to be sure about more than that? That's him. That's the man. You can't be mistaken about that. I know that face anywhere. I know that nose, and I know those colored eyes!"

Frank Locke swung back toward the door. His lips were snarling. "Say," he said, "what kind of a double-cross am I getting here, anyway? What sort of frame-up is this? This won't buy you anything. You'll get the works for this!"

"Keep your shirt on," Mason told him, then turned to the pawnbroker.

"Sol," he said, "you've got to be so absolutely certain about this that you can go on the witness stand and no amount of cross-examination can shake your testimony."

Sol waved expressive palms under his chin. "How could I be more certain?" he said. "Put me on the witness stand. Bring me on a dozen lawyers. Bring me on a hundred lawyers! I'll tell the same story."

Frank Locke said, "I never saw this man in my life."

Sol Steinburg's laugh was a masterpiece of sarcastic merriment.

Little beads of perspiration were showing on Locke's forehead. He turned to Mason.

"What's the idea?" he said. "What sort of a flim-flam is this?"

Mason shook his head gravely.

"It's just a part of my case," he said. "It checks up, that's all."

"What checks up?"

"The fact that you bought the gun," Mason said, in a low voice.

144

"You're crazy as hell!" Locke yelled. "I never bought a gun here in my life. I never was inside the place. I never saw the store. I don't carry a gun!"

Mason said to Steinburg, "Give me your gun register, will you, Sol? Then beat it. I want to talk."

Steinburg passed over the booklet, waddled to the back of the store.

Mason opened the book to the place where the 32-automatic Colt had been noted. He held the palm of his hand casually, so that the number of the gun was partially covered. With his forefinger, he indicated the words "32-Colt automatic." Then he moved over toward the name which was on the margin.

"I presume you'll deny that you wrote that?" he asked.

Locke seemed trying to tear himself away, yet to be held by some impelling curiosity. He leaned forward. "Certainly I deny that I wrote it. I never was in the joint. I never saw this man. I never bought a gun here, and that isn't my signature."

Mason said, patiently, "I know it isn't your signature, Locke. But are you going to say that you didn't write it? You'd better be careful, because it may make quite a difference."

"Of course I didn't write it. What the hell's eating you?"

"The police don't know it yet," said Mason, "but that gun is the one that killed George Belter last night."

Locke recoiled as though he had been struck a blow. His milk-chocolate eyes were wide and wild. The glint of the perspiration on his forehead was quite evident now.

"So that's the kind of a dirty damn frame-up this is, is it?"

"Now, wait a minute, Locke," Mason cautioned. "Don't fly off the handle. I could have gone to the police with this thing, but I didn't. I'm just working it my own way. I'm going to give you the breaks."

"It'll take more than you and a crooked pawnbroker to

145

frame anything like that on me," Locke snarled. "Just for this I'm going to blow the lid off!"

Mason's voice remained calm and patient. "Well, let's go out where we can talk a bit. I want to talk where we won't have any witnesses."

"You just steered me in here on a frame-up. That's what I get for going with you. Now you can go to hell!"

"I steered you in here so Sol could take a good look at you," Mason told him. "That's all. He told me that he'd know the man if he ever saw him again. I had to be sure."

Locke backed toward the door.

"What a sweet frame-up this is," he said. "If you'd gone to the cops with a story like that, they'd have made you put me in a line of men, and seen whether or not he could have picked me out of the line. But you didn't do that. You brought me in here. How do I know that you haven't slipped this fellow some money to pull this stunt?"

Mason laughed.

"If you want to go down to police headquarters and get in a line of men, I'll take you down there. And I guess Sol can pick you out," he said.

"Of course he can, now that you've put the finger on me."

"Well," Mason said, "we're not getting anywhere with this. Come on, let's go outside."

He took Locke's arm and piloted him through the door.

In the street, Locke turned to him savagely, and said, "I'm finished with you. I'm not saying a damned word. I'm going back to the office, and you can go to hell!"

"That wouldn't be a very wise course of procedure, Locke," Mason said, holding Locke's arm. "You see, I've got a motive for the crime, opportunity, and everything."

"Yes?" sneered Locke. "What's your motive? I'm interested in that."

"You have been embezzling funds from the Extraordinary Expense Account," said Mason, "and you were afraid of discovery. You didn't dare to cross Belter be-

146

cause he knew too much about that Savannah affair. He could have sent you back on a murder rap. So you went out there and had an argument with him, and killed him."

Locke was staring at Mason. He had ceased walking, and stood stock-still, his face white, his lips quivering. A blow in the stomach would not have jarred him more. He tried to speak and could not.

Mason was elaborately casual. "Now I want to be fair, Locke," he went on. "And I think that he is on the square. If it is a frame-up they won't convict you. You've got to prove that a man's guilty beyond a reasonable doubt, you know. And if you can raise even a reasonable doubt, a jury is duty bound to return a verdict of not guilty."

Locke found his voice. "Where do you come in on this?" he asked.

Mason shrugged his shoulders. "I'm counsel for Eva Belter," he said. "That's all."

Locke tried to sneer but it didn't get across very well. "So she's in on this too! You've teamed up with that two-timing broad!"

"She's my client, if that's what you mean."

"That isn't what I mean," Locke said.

Mason's voice became hard. "It might be a good plan for you to keep your mouth shut then, Locke. You're attracting attention. People are looking at you."

Locke controlled himself with an effort.

"Listen," he said, "I don't know what your game is, but I'm going to spike it right now. I've got an absolute iron-clad alibi for last night at the time when that murder was committed, and just to show you where you stand, I'm going to spring it on you."

Mason shrugged his shoulders.

"Okay," he said, "spring it on me."

Locke looked up and down the street. "All right, we get a taxicab."

"Fine," said Mason, "we get a taxicab."

A cab caught Locke's signal, pulled into the curb. Locke

said, "Wheelright Hotel," climbed in and settled back in the cushions. He mopped his forehead with a handkerchief, lit a cigarette with a hand that trembled, and turned to Mason.

"Listen," he said, "you're a man of the world. I'm going to take you to a young lady's room. I don't want her name brought into this. I don't know what your game is, but I'm just going to show you how little chance you'd stand of making this frame-up stick."

"You don't need to prove that it's a frame-up, you know, Locke. All you've got to do is to raise a reasonable doubt. If you could raise a reasonable doubt, why, there isn't a jury on earth that would convict you."

Locke slammed the cigarette to the floor of the car. "For God's sake, cut out that damned talk! I know what you're trying to do, and you know what you're trying to do. You're trying to break my nerve and get my goat. What the hell's the use of beating around the bush? You're trying to pin something on me, and I don't propose to stand for it."

"What are you getting so worked up for if it's a frame-up?"

"Because," Locke said, "I'm afraid of some of the stuff you might bring up."

"You mean that Savannah stuff?"

Locke cursed, turned his head so that Mason couldn't see his face, and looked out of the cab window.

Mason sat back, apparently entirely absorbed in the crowds on the sidewalks, the fronts of the buildings, the window displays.

Locke started to say something once, but changed his mind and lapsed into silence. His milk-chocolate eyes were wide and worried. His face had not regained its color. It showed white and pasty.

The cab drew up in front of the Wheelright Hotel.

Locke got out and indicated Mason to the cab driver, with a gesture of his hand.

Mason shook his head.

"No, Locke," he said, "this is your party. You wanted the cab."

Locke pulled a bill out of his pocket, tossed it to the cab driver, turned, and started through the entrance of the hotel. Mason followed.

Locke walked at once to the elevator, said, "Ninth floor," to the operator.

When the cage stopped, he got out and walked straight toward Esther Linten's room, without bothering to see if Mason was following. He knocked on the door. "It's me, Honey," he called.

Esther Linten opened the door. She had on a kimono which opened in the front sufficiently to reveal pink silk underwear. When she saw Mason, she pulled the kimono abruptly about her, and stepped back, her eyes large.

"What's the meaning of this, Frank?" she asked.

Locke pushed on past her. "I can't explain things, Honey, but I want you to tell this fellow where I was last night."

She lowered her eyes, and said, "What do you mean, Frank?"

Locke's voice was savage. "Oh, nix on that stuff. You know what I mean. Go on. This is a jam, and you've got to come clean."

She stared at Locke with fluttering eyelids. *"Tell him everything?"* she asked.

"Everything," said Locke. "He ain't a vice squad. He's just a dumb boob that thinks he can work a frame-up on me, and get away with it."

She spoke, in a low voice, "We went out, and after that, you came here."

"Then what happened?" pressed Locke.

"I undressed," she muttered.

"Go on," said Locke. "Tell it to him. Give him the whole business. Speak up so he can hear you."

"I went to bed," she said slowly, "and I'd had a couple of drinks."

"What time was that?" asked Mason.

"About eleven-thirty, I guess," she said.

Locke stared at her. "What happened after that?" he demanded.

She shook her head. "I woke up this morning with an awful headache, Frank. And I knew, of course, that you were here when I went to sleep. But I don't know what time you went out, or anything about it. I passed out after I got into bed."

Locke jumped away from her and stood in a corner, as though he were guarding himself against a physical attack from both of them.

"You dirty, double-crossing . . ."

Mason interrupted, "That's no way to talk to a lady."

Locke was furious. "You damn fool. Can't you see she ain't a lady?"

Esther Linten stared at him from angry eyes. *"That's* not going to get you anywhere, Frank. If you didn't want me to tell the truth, why the hell didn't you tell me you wanted an alibi? If you'd wanted me to lie about it why didn't you tip me off, and I'd have said anything you wanted me to say. But you told me to tell the truth and I did."

Locke cursed again.

"Well," said the lawyer, "it's very evident that this young lady is dressing. We don't want to detain her. I'm in a hurry, Locke. Do you want to go with me, or do you want to stay here with her?"

Locke's tone was ominous as he said, "I'll stay here with her."

"Fine," Mason remarked, "I'll put in a telephone call from here."

He walked over to the telephone, took down the receiver, and said, "Police Headquarters."

150

Locke watched him with the look of a cornered rat in his eyes.

After a while Mason spoke into the transmitter, "Get me Sidney Drumm, will you? He's on the Detective Force."

Locke's voice rasped out in agony, "For God's sake, hang up that receiver, quick."

Mason turned to survey him with mild curiosity.

"Hang it up!" yelled Locke. "Damn it, you've got the whip hand. You've worked a frame-up on me that I can't buck. Not that the frame-up isn't crude as hell, but I don't dare to have you go into the motive. That's the thing that cooks me. You put on evidence about the motive and a jury would never listen to anything else."

Mason slid the receiver back on the hook, turned to face Locke.

"Now," he said, "we're getting some place."

"What is it you want?" asked Locke.

"You know what I want," said Mason.

Locke flung out his hands in a gesture of surrender.

"All right," he said, "that's understood. Anything else?"

Mason shook his head. "Not right now. It might be well to remember that Eva Belter is the real owner of the paper now. Personally, I think it would be a good plan to consult with her before you publish *anything* which might be distasteful to her. You come out every two weeks, don't you?"

"Yes, our publication day is next Thursday."

"Anything may happen between now and then, Locke," Mason told him.

Locke said nothing.

Mason turned to the girl.

"I'm sorry we disturbed you, Miss," he said.

"That's all right," she said. "If the damn fool wanted me to lie, why didn't he say so? What was his idea in telling me he wanted me to tell the truth?"

Locke whirled on her. "You *are* lying, Esther. You

151

know damned well you didn't pass out when you went to bed."

She shrugged her shoulders.

"Maybe I didn't," she said, "but I can't remember anything. Lots of times when I get plastered, I can't remember what happened all during that evening."

Locke said meaningly, "Well, you'd better get over that habit. It might prove fatal."

She flared at him. "I should think you'd have a bellyful of having friends who had things fatal happen to them!"

He went white. "Shut up, Esther. Can't you get the sketch?"

"Shut up yourself, then! I'm not a girl that you can talk to that way."

Mason interposed. "Well, never mind, it's all settled now, anyway. Come on, Locke, let's get going. I think you'd better come with me after all. I've got some more things I want to say to you."

Locke walked to the door, paused, looked at Esther Linten with his mild brown eyes gleaming malevolence, and then stepped out into the corridor.

Mason stepped up behind him without even looking back at the girl, and closed the door. He took Locke's arm and piloted him toward the elevator.

"I just want you to know," said Locke, "that that frame-up was so damned crude that it wasn't even funny. It was this Georgia business that you mentioned that bothered me. I don't want to have anybody go into that. I think you've got the wrong idea about it, but it's something that's a closed chapter in my life."

Mason smiled, and said, "Oh, no, it isn't, Locke. Murder never outlaws, you know, and they can always bring you back for another trial."

Locke pushed himself away from Mason's side. His lips were twitching, and his eyes were filled with panic. "I can beat that case if they try me in Savannah. But if you spring it here in connection with another murder case, they'd make short work of me, and you're just smooth enough to know it."

Mason shrugged his shoulders. "Incidentally, Locke," he said, "I presume that you've been embezzling money from the accounts to keep this thing going," and he jerked his thumb back toward the room they had quitted.

"Well," said Locke, "guess again. That's one place where you can't do a damn thing. Nobody on earth knows what my understanding was with George Belter, except George Belter. It wasn't in writing. It was just an understanding between us."

"Well, be careful what you say, Locke," Mason warned, "and remember that Mrs. Belter is the owner of the paper now. You'd better have an understanding with her before you pay out any *more* money. Your accounts will have to be audited in court now, you know."

Locke swore under his breath. "So that's it, is it?"

"That's it," Mason said. "I'm going to leave you when we get out of the hotel, Locke. Don't go back and try to beat up that woman, because anything she might say wouldn't make a particle of difference. I don't know whether Sol Steinburg is right in identifying you as the man who bought the murder gun in this case or not. But, even if he isn't, all we need to do is to simply pass the word to the Georgia authorities, and you go back for another trial. Maybe you beat the rap, maybe you don't; but you're out of the picture here."

Locke said, curiously, "Listen, you're playing a hell of a deep game. I'd like to know what it is."

Mason looked at him innocently.

"Why no, Locke," he said, "I'm just representing a client, and sort of messing around here, trying to find out something. I had some detectives who chased down the number on the gun. I guess we got it a little bit in advance of the police, because they are going about it as a matter of routine. And I did some single-shooting on it."

Locke laughed. "Save that," he said, "and tell it to

153

somebody who appreciates it. You don't fool me any with that damned innocent stuff."

Mason shrugged his shoulders.

"Well, Locke," he said, "I'm sorry. I may get in touch with you later on. In the meantime, I'd be awfully careful about mentioning anything at all about Mrs. Belter's business, or about my business, and that goes double for anything connected with this Beechwood Inn business, or Harrison Burke."

"Hell," said Locke, "you don't need to rub it in. I'm off of that stuff for life. I know when I'm licked. What are you going to do about that Georgia business? Anything?"

"I'm not a detective or an officer. I'm simply a lawyer. I'm representing Mrs. Belter. That's all."

The cage dropped them into the lobby of the hotel, and Mason went to the door and signaled a taxi.

"So long, Locke," he said. "I'll see you later."

As the cab drove away, Locke was standing in the doorway, leaning up against the building for support. His face was pale and his lips twisted into a frozen smile.

15

PERRY MASON SAT IN HIS ROOM AT THE HOTEL. THERE were dark circles under his eyes, and his face was gray with fatigue. The eyes, however, were steady in their calm concentration, dominating the entire face.

Morning sunlight was streaming in through the windows. The bed was littered with newspapers. Headlines streamed across them news of the Belter murder, which had developed enough interesting angles to betray to the news-skilled reporters that a major sensation was due to break.

The *Examiner* carried headlines which monopolized the front page. "MURDER BARES ROMANCE." Underneath in smaller headlines: "NEPHEW OF VICTIM ENGAGED TO HOUSEKEEPER'S DAUGHTER. SECRET ROMANCE BARED BY POLICE.—WILL CONTEST FILED IN BELTER ESTATE. DISINHERITED WIDOW CLAIMS WILL FORGERY—POLICE TRACE GUN TO MISSING MAN—WIDOW'S CHANCE REMARK STARTS SEARCH FOR LAWYER."

These headlines appeared over different articles on the front page of the paper. The inside page showed pictures of Eva Belter sitting with her knees crossed, a handkerchief to her eyes. There were headlines with the by-line of a well-known sob sister, "WIDOW WEEPS AS POLICE QUESTION."

Reading the newspapers, Mason had kept abreast of the situation. He had learned that the police had traced the gun to one Pete Mitchell, who had mysteriously disappeared immediately after the shooting, but who had a perfect alibi covering the time when the crime had actually been committed. It was the assumption of the police that Mitchell was shielding some one to whom he had given the gun.

No names were mentioned, but Mason was able to realize that the police were getting close to Harrison Burke. He had also read, with increasing interest, about a chance remark which Eva Belter had made which had caused the police to start seeking an attorney who had represented her, and who had mysteriously disappeared from his office. The police were confidently predicting that the mystery would be solved within another twenty-four hours, and the man who fired the fatal shot be behind the bars.

Somebody knocked at the door.

Perry Mason put down the newspaper he was reading, cocked his head on one side, and listened.

The knock was repeated.

Mason shrugged his shoulders, walked to the door, twisted the key, and opened it.

Della Street was in the hall.

She pushed her way into the room, slammed the door behind her, and locked it.

"I told you not to risk it," Mason told her.

She turned around and looked at him. Her eyes were slightly blood-shot, with dark circles under them, and her face was haggard.

"I don't care," she said. "It was all right. I managed to ditch them. I've been playing tag with them for an hour."

"You can't ever tell about those fellows, Della. They're clever. Sometimes they let you think you've got away in order to find out where you wanted to go."

"They didn't slip anything over on me," she said in a voice that told of raw nerves. "I tell you they don't know where I am."

He caught the note of hysteria in her voice. "Well, I'm glad you're here. I was just wondering who I could get to take down some stuff."

"What stuff?"

"Some stuff that's going to come up."

She made a gesture toward the newspapers on the bed.

"Chief," she said, "I told you that she was going to get you into trouble. She came into the office and signed those papers. There were a bunch of reporters hanging around, of course, and they started going after her. Then the detectives took her down to Headquarters for further questioning. You can see what she did."

Mason nodded. "That's all right. Don't get excited, Della."

"Get excited? Do you know what she did? She made the statement down there that she recognized your voice. That *you* were the man that was in the room with Belter when the shot was fired. And then she pulled a fainting fit, and a lot of hysterics, and stuff of that sort."

156

"That's all right, Della," he said soothingly. "I knew she was going to do that."

Della stared at him with wide eyes.

"*You* did?" she asked. "I thought *I* was the one who knew that!"

He nodded. "Sure you did, Della. So did I."

"She's a rat and a liar!" Della Street said.

Mason shrugged his shoulders and walked to the telephone. He gave the number of Drake's Detective Bureau, and got Paul Drake on the line.

"Listen, Paul," he said, "make sure you're not tailed, and sneak over to Room 518 in the Hotel Ripley. Better bring a couple of stenographer's notebooks, and a bunch of pencils along with you. Will you?"

"Right away?" asked the detective.

"Right away," he said. "It's eight forty-five now, and I'm expecting a show to start at nine."

He hung up the telephone.

Della Street was curious. "What is it, chief?" she asked.

"I'm expecting Eva Belter to be here at nine o'clock," he said briefly.

"I don't want to be here when that woman's here," Della Street said. "I can't trust myself around her. She's double-crossed you all the way from the start. I want to kill her. She's such a sleek little gutter rat."

He put his hand on her shoulder. "Sit down and take it easy, Della. There's going to be a show-down."

There was a sound at the door. The knob turned, the door opened, and Eva Belter walked in.

She looked at Della Street, and said, "Oh, you're *both* here."

"Apparently," Mason said, "you've been doing some talking." He gestured, as he spoke, toward the newspapers which were piled on the bed.

She walked over to him, ignoring the other woman, placed her hands on his shoulders, looked up in his eyes. "Perry," she said, "I never felt so rotten about anything in

157

my life. I don't know how I happened to say it. They got me down at Headquarters and barked questions at me. Everybody shrieked questions. I never saw anything like it. I didn't dream that it would be anything at all like that. I tried to protect you, but I couldn't. It slipped out, and just as soon as I made the first slip, they all started piling on me. They made threats, and told me they'd name me as an accessory."

"What did you tell them?" asked Mason.

She looked in his eyes, then went over to the bed, sat down, took out her handkerchief from her purse, and started to cry.

Della Street moved two swift steps toward her, but Mason caught her arm and pushed her back.

"I'm handling this," he said.

Eva Belter continued to sob into her handkerchief.

"Go ahead," said Mason. "What did you tell them?"

She shook her head.

"Never mind that sob stuff," he said, "it doesn't go over so big right now. We're in a jam and you'd better tell me what you said."

She sobbed. "I just t-t-t-told them that I heard your v-v-v-voice."

"Did you say it was my voice? Or some one that sounded like me?"

"I t-t-told them everything. That it *was* your voice."

His tone was hard. "You knew damned well it wasn't my voice."

"I didn't intend to tell them," she wailed, "but it was the truth. It was your voice."

"All right. We'll take it that way," Mason said.

Della Street started to say something, but stopped when he turned on her and fastened her with level-lidded eyes.

There was a silence in the room, broken only by the faint rumble of noises from the street, and the sobs of the woman.

After a minute or two the door opened, and Paul Drake walked in.

"Hello, everybody," he said, cheerfully. "Made time, didn't I? I got a break. There was nobody who seemed to have the slightest interest in where I was, or what I was doing."

"Did you see anybody hanging around the front of the place?" asked Mason. "I'm not entirely certain that they didn't shadow Della."

"Nobody that I noticed."

Mason waved his hand toward the woman who sat on the bed with her legs crossed.

"This is Eva Belter," he said.

Drake grinned and looked at the legs.

"Yes," he said, "I recognized her from a picture in the paper."

Eva Belter took the handkerchief down from her eyes, and stared up at Drake. She smiled ingratiatingly.

Della Street snapped, "Even your tears weren't genuine!"

Eva Belter turned and looked at her, her blue eyes suddenly grown hard.

Perry Mason whirled on Della. "Listen, Della," he said, "I'm running this show." He looked over at Paul Drake. "Did you bring the notebooks and pencils, Paul?"

The detective nodded.

Mason took the notebooks and pencils, and passed them over to Della Street.

"Can you move the table and take down what's said, Della?" he asked.

"I can try," she said in a choked voice.

"All right. Be sure and get what *she* says," and he jerked his thumb in the direction of Eva Belter.

Eva Belter looked from one to the other. "What is it?" she asked. "What are you doing?"

"I'm going to get the straight of this," Mason told her.

"You want *me* here?" asked Paul Drake.

159

"Sure," Mason told him. "You're a witness."

"You make me nervous," said Eva Belter. "That's the way they did last night. They had me in the District Attorney's office, and they had people sitting there with notebooks and pencils. It makes me nervous to have people take down what I say."

Mason smiled. "Yes, I should think it would. Did they ask you anything about the gun?"

Eva Belter widened her blue eyes in that stare of innocence which made her seem so young and helpless.

"What do you mean?" she asked.

"You know what I mean," Mason persisted. "Did they ask anything about how you happened to have the gun?"

"How *I* happened to have the gun?" she asked.

"Yes," said Mason. "Harrison Burke gave it to you, you know, and that's the reason you had to telephone him—to tell him that it was his gun that had been used in the shooting."

Della Street's pencil was skipping rapidly over the page of the notebook.

"I'm sure I don't know what you're talking about," Eva Belter said with dignity.

"Oh, yes, you do," Mason told her. "You telephoned Burke that there had been an accident or something, and that his gun had figured in it. He'd had the gun given him by a friend named Mitchell, and he drove right around and picked up Mitchell. The two of them ducked under cover."

"Why," she exclaimed, "I never heard of anything like that!"

"That line isn't going to get you anywhere, Eva," Mason told her, "because I saw Harrison Burke, and I have a statement signed by him."

She stiffened in sudden consternation.

"*You* have a statement signed by *him?*" she asked.

"Yes."

"I thought you were representing *me*."

160

"What's wrong with representing you and having a statement from Burke?" he asked.

"Nothing, only he's lying if he said that he ever gave me that gun. I never saw it in my life."

"That makes it more simple," Mason commented.

"What does?"

"You'll see," he told her. "Now let's go back and clear up another point or two. When you got your purse it was in your husband's desk. Do you remember that?"

"What do you mean?" she inquired in a low cautious voice.

"When I was there with you," Mason said, "and you got your purse."

"Oh, yes, I remember that! I'd put it in the desk earlier in the evening."

"Fine," said Mason. "Now, just between the four of us, who do you *think* was in the room with your husband when the shot was fired?"

She said simply, "You were."

"That's fine," Mason said without enthusiasm. "Now, your husband had been taking a bath just before the shot was fired."

For the first time she seemed uneasy. "I don't know about that. You were there. I wasn't."

"Yes, you know," Mason insisted. "He was in the bath, and he got out and put a bathrobe around him, without even waiting to dry himself."

"Did he?" she asked mechanically.

"You know he did, and the evidence shows he did. Now, how do you suppose that *I* got in to see him if he was in his bath?"

"Why, I guess the servant let you in, didn't he?"

Mason smiled. "The servant doesn't say so, does he?"

"Well, I don't know. All I know is that I heard your voice."

"You'd been out with Burke," Mason said, slowly, "and

161

you came in. You didn't carry your purse with you while you were wearing your evening clothes, did you?"

"No, I didn't have it with me then," she said, and suddenly bit her lip.

Mason grinned at her.

"Then how," he said, "did it get in your husband's desk?"

"I don't know."

"You remember the receipts that I gave you for the amounts you paid on account of fees?" Mason asked.

She nodded her head.

"Where are they?"

She shrugged her shoulders.

"I don't know," she said, "I've lost them."

"That," Mason said, "clinches it."

"Clinches what?" she asked.

"The fact that you killed him. You won't tell me what happened, so *I'll* tell *you* what happened.

"You had been out with Burke. You came in, and Burke left you at the door. You went upstairs, and your husband heard you coming. He was in the bath at the time. He was in a towering rage. He jumped out of the bath, threw the robe around him, and called to you to come into his suite. You went in there and he showed you the two receipts that he'd found in your purse while you were out. They had my name on them. I'd been there and told him what it was that I was trying to keep out of *Spicy Bits*. He put two and two together, and knew who it was that I was representing right then."

"Why I never heard of such a thing!" she said.

He grinned at her. "Oh, yes, you did! You knew that it was a show-down right then, and you shot him. He fell, and you rushed out of the place, but you played it pretty smooth at that. You dropped the gun on the floor, knowing that it could be traced to Harrison Burke and could never be traced any farther. You wanted to get Harrison Burke in it, so that he'd have to get you out. And you

162

wanted to get me in it for the same reason. You went down and telephoned Burke and told him that something had happened, and that his gun would be found, that he'd better get out and lie low, and that his only hope was to keep sending me plenty of money so that I would go ahead with the case.

"Then you telephoned to me and got me to come out there. You told me that you recognized my voice as the voice of the man who was in the room with your husband because you wanted my help, and also because you wanted to fix it so that I couldn't prove an alibi if you wanted to spring this business about recognizing my voice in the apartment.

"You figured that if you could drag me and Harrison Burke both into the mess, we'd get you out while we were getting ourselves out. You figured that I'd get busy and square the thing some way, with Burke's money back of me, and the fact that I was in a jam to spur me on.

"You figured that you could pretend you didn't realize just how much you had me in your power by saying that you recognized my voice as that of the man in the room with your husband.

"Also, you figured that if you got in a position where they commenced to put the screws on you, you'd switch the whole thing to me, and let Burke and me fight it out between us."

She was staring at him now her face chalk-white, her eyes dark with panic.

"You've got no right to talk that way," she charged.

"The hell I haven't!" he said. "I've got proof."

"What kind of proof?"

He laughed harshly. "What do you think I was doing all the time you were being questioned last night?" he said. "I got in touch with Harrison Burke, and we got in touch with the housekeeper. The housekeeper was trying to protect you, but she knows that you came in with Burke and that your husband called to you as you went upstairs. She

163

knows that he was looking for you earlier in the evening, and that he had your purse, and had found the two receipts with my signature on them.

"When you had the receipts made out without any name on them, you thought it would be all right. But you forgot that *my* name was signed to them, and that as soon as your husband knew the case that I was working on and found the receipts in your purse, he knew that you were the woman in the case."

Her face was twisting now. "You're my lawyer. You can't use all of the things that I've told you to build up a case against me. You've got to be loyal to my interests."

He laughed bitterly.

"I suppose I should sit tight and let you drag *me* into the murder, so that you can walk out, eh?"

"I didn't say that. I just want you to be loyal to me."

"You're a hell of a person to talk of loyalty."

She tried another defense. "All that is a mess of lies," she charged, "and you can't prove it."

Perry Mason reached for his hat.

"Maybe I can't prove it," he said, "but you put in the night making wild statements to the District Attorney. *I'm* going down and make a statement now. When I get done they'll have a pretty good idea of the real facts of the case. What with telephoning to Harrison Burke about the gun, and telling him to get out, and the motive that you had in order to keep your husband from discovering your affair with Burke, the police will have a pretty good case."

"But I didn't gain anything by his death."

"That's another slick thing," he said coldly, "that is just like everything else you did. It's just slick enough to look good on the face, but not clever enough to really get by. The forgery of that will was a good job."

"What do you mean?"

"Exactly what I said," he snapped. "Your husband told you that you were disinherited, or else you found the will in his safe. At any rate, you knew the terms of the will, and you knew where it was kept. You tried to figure some way of getting around that will. You knew that if you destroyed it, it wouldn't do you any good because Carl Griffin and Arthur Atwood, his lawyer, had seen the will, and that your husband had told them about it. If it was missing they'd suspect you.

"But you figured that if you could trap Griffin into claiming under the will and then prove that the will was a forgery, you'd have Griffin in a questionable position. So you went ahead and forged the will that your husband had drawn, making the forgery crude enough to be easily detected, but copying the will word for word. Then you planted your forged will where you could get it whenever you wanted to.

"When you had me at the house, examining the body, you pretended to be overcome with emotion. You wouldn't come near the body. But while I was busy looking things over, you got the original will and destroyed it. You planted your forged copy. Naturally Griffin and his lawyer walked into the trap and claimed that the will was the original holographic will of George Belter, because they knew the terms of the genuine will.

"As a matter of fact, it's such a clumsy forgery, that they can't even get a handwriting expert to testify that it's genuine. They realize now the position that they're in, but they've already filed the will and made affidavits to the effect that it's genuine. They don't dare to back up. It's pretty slick."

She got slowly to her feet.

"You've got to have some proof of this," she said, but her tone was thin and trembling.

Mason nodded his head to Drake.

"Go in the next room, Drake," he said. "You'll find Mrs. Veitch in there. Bring her out and let her corroborate what I've said."

Drake's face was like a mask. He got up and walked to

the communicating door which led to the adjoining room. He opened it.

"Mrs. Veitch," he called.

There was a rustle of motion.

Mrs. Veitch, tall, bony, dressed in black, walked into the room with her lack-luster eyes staring straight ahead.

"Good morning," she said to Eva Belter.

Perry Mason suddenly said, "Just one moment, Mrs. Veitch. There's one other matter I want to clear up before I have you make your statement to Mrs. Belter. If you'll just step back in the other room for a moment, please."

Mrs. Veitch turned and walked back to the room.

Paul Drake flashed Perry Mason a quizzical glance, and shut the door.

Eva Belter took two steps toward the outer door, then suddenly toppled forward.

Perry Mason caught her as she pitched forward.

Drake came up and took her legs. Together, they carried her to the bed, and laid her down.

Della Street laid down her pencil, gave a little exclamation, and pushed back her chair.

Mason turned on her almost savagely.

"Stay there!" he said. "Take down everything that's said! Don't miss a word!"

He went to the washstand, sopped a towel in cold water, and slapped it down on Eva Belter's face. They loosened the front of her dress, and slapped her chest with the towel.

She gasped and recovered consciousness.

She looked up at Mason, and said, "Please, Perry, help me."

He shook his head. "I can't help you," he said, "as long as you're trying to give me the double-cross."

"I'll come clean," she wailed.

"All right. What happened?"

"Just what you said, only I didn't know Mrs. Veitch

knew about it. I didn't know any one heard George call me or heard the shot."

"How close to him were you when you shot him?"

"I was way across the room," she answered tonelessly. "Honestly, I didn't intend to do it. I just shot him on impulse. I had the gun to use for defense in the event he should attack me. I was afraid he'd try to kill me. He had a violent temper, and I knew that if he ever found out about Harrison Burke, he'd do something awful. As soon as I knew he'd found out, I slipped the gun into my hand. When he started for me, I screamed and shot. I guess I dropped the gun right there on the floor. I wasn't certain about it at the time. Honestly, the idea of getting Burke into it never occurred to me then. I was too rattled to think of anything. I simply ran out into the night.

"I'm not a fool, and I knew how black things would look for me, particularly in view of the mess that I was in with Harrison Burke on account of the Beechwood Inn murder.

"I just ran blindly out into the rain and didn't have very much of an idea what I was doing. I remember grabbing a coat as I went past the hall stand. But it shows how rattled I was that I didn't even take my own coat. It was there, but I grabbed an old overcoat that Carl Griffin sometimes wore. I threw it around me and kept running. After a while I got my wits about me and decided that I'd better call you. I didn't know then whether or not he was dead. But I knew that if I was going to have to face him, I wanted to have you with me.

"He didn't run after me, so I was afraid that I'd killed him. It really wasn't premeditated. It was just on impulse. He'd found my purse and gone through it. That was a habit he had, looking for letters. I wasn't foolish enough to have any letters in there, but I did have those receipts, and he put two and two together.

"He was taking a bath when I came in. He heard me, I guess. He climbed out of the bathtub, and threw the bathrobe around him, and started bellowing for me. I went up there and he had the receipts. He accused me of being the woman who was with Harrison Burke, and then he accused me of a lot of things, and said that he was going to throw me out without a penny. I became hysterical, and grabbed the gun and shot him. After I got down to the drug store, and was ready to telephone you, I realized that I was going to need somebody to stand back of me. I didn't have any money of my own. I told you that. My husband kept all the money, and only gave me a little at a time. I knew about the will that was made out in favor of Carl Griffin, and I was afraid that I couldn't get any money out of the estate while it was being tied up in probate. I knew that Harrison Burke would be afraid of getting his name mixed into the thing, and that he'd leave me flat. I had to have money; I had to have somebody to stand back of me. So I rang up Harrison Burke and deliberately mixed him into it. I told him that something had happened, and that his gun had figured in it. That I didn't know who the man was that had killed him, but I did know that his gun was on the floor.

"It was a stall that wouldn't have gone over with you, but it went over with Burke all right. Burke was frantic.

"I told him there was only one thing to do, and that was for him to get under cover, and fix it so they couldn't trace the gun to him, if he could. And in the meantime, to see that you had plenty of money to go ahead and do anything that you could. Then I telephoned you and got you to come over.

"While you were driving down there, I got to thinking how much better it would be if I could have you in a position where you were forced to get me out of it in order to save yourself, and also, have some kind of an explanation that I could make to the police if the police should start suspecting me.

"You were right about that." She went on, "I knew that they could never convict you, because you were too smart

168

and skillful. *You* could get out of it, and I figured that if they got to crowding me too close, I'd give them the information that I did, so that they'd go after you and that would clear me. If they ever tried to come back on me after you had drawn their fire, I knew that it would be an easy case to beat."

Mason looked up at Paul Drake and shook his head.

"Nice little playmate, isn't she?" he said.

There was a knock at the door.

Mason looked at the occupants of the room. Then tiptoed to the door, and opened it.

Sidney Drumm stood on the threshold. There was another man back of him.

"Hello, Perry," he said. "We had a devil of a time finding you. We trailed Della Street to this hotel, but it took us quite a little while to find out what alias you were registered under. I'm sorry to bother you, but you've got to take a little ride with me. The District Attorney wants to ask you a few questions."

Mason nodded. "Walk right in," he said.

Eva Belter gave a little cry. "Perry, you've got to protect me! I came clean. You've got to stand back of me."

Perry looked at her, then turned abruptly to Sidney Drumm.

"This is a break for you, Sidney," he said. "You're going to be able to make the arrest. This is Eva Belter, who has just confessed to the murder of her husband."

Eva Belter screamed, got to her feet and swayed uncertainly.

Drumm looked from one to the other.

"It's a fact," Paul Drake said.

Mason motioned toward Della Street.

"It's all down there," he said, "in black and white. We've got witnesses, and we've got her statement taken verbatim."

Sidney Drumm whistled under his breath.

"By God, Perry," he said, "that's a lucky break for you! They were going to charge *you* with the murder."

Mason's voice was savage, "There wasn't any luck about it. I was willing to give her a break as long as she shot square. But when I read in the paper about her dragging me into it, I made up my mind that I was going to call for a show-down."

Paul Drake said, "Do you really know where Harrison Burke is?"

"Hell, no!" said Perry Mason. "I didn't even get out of this room last night. I simply sat here and thought. I did get hold of Mrs. Veitch, and told her that Eva Belter was going to be in here this morning and wanted her to be here in order to corroborate a statement she was going to make to the reporters. I sent a taxi out for Mrs. Veitch and had her come in."

"She wouldn't have backed you up in the statement?" asked Drake.

"I don't know," said Mason. "I don't think so. I didn't talk with her at all. She wouldn't talk with me. I think she's holding something back, though. I'm satisfied she knows something. I simply wanted to have you open the door and let Eva Belter see her here for the purpose of exerting a little pressure."

Eva Belter stared white-faced at Perry Mason.

"Damn you," she said, "for a double-crossing back-stabber!"

It was Sidney Drumm who gave the situation its last touch of irony. "Hell," he said, "Eva Belter was the woman who told us where you were, Perry. She said she was going to see you this morning and that we could wait until someone else came here and claim we'd followed that other person. She wanted to have you think we'd followed Della Street or someone, instead of her."

Mason made no comment. His face was suddenly very weary.

16

PERRY MASON SAT IN HIS OFFICE LOOKING VERY TIRED.

Della Street sat across the desk from him and avoided his eyes.

"I thought you didn't like her," Mason remarked.

She kept her eyes averted.

"I didn't," she admitted, "but I'm sorry that you had to be the one that made the disclosure. She relied on you to get her out of trouble. You turned her over to the officers."

"I didn't do anything of the sort," he denied. "I simply refused to be the goat."

She shrugged her shoulders.

"I've known you quite a long time," Della said, slowly. "During that time your clients have always come first. You didn't make the cases, and you didn't make the clients. You took them as they came. More often than not the cases seemed pretty hopeless. But while you represented them, you never went back on any client. You never stopped fighting."

"What is this," he asked, "a sermon?"

"Yes," she said, shortly.

"Go on, then."

She shook her head.

"It's finished."

He got up and walked over to her, and put his hand on her shoulder.

"Della," he said, "I've got one thing to ask you."

171

"What is it?"

"Please have confidence in me," he said, humbly.

She looked up and met his eyes then.

"You mean . . . ?"

He nodded his head.

"She isn't convicted," he said, "of a damned thing until a jury brings in a verdict finding her guilty of something."

"But," said Della Street, "she won't have anything more to do with you. She'll get another lawyer now, and she's confessed. How are you going to get away from that confession? She repeated the confession to the police and signed it."

"I don't have to get away from it. You've got to convict them beyond a reasonable doubt. If a jury has a reasonable doubt, it can't convict. I can get her free yet."

She scowled at him.

"Why couldn't you have let Paul Drake tip off the police to ask her certain questions?" she said. "Why did *you* have to tell them?"

"Because she'd have lied her way out of any questions the police could have asked. She's clever, that woman. She wanted me to help her, but she figured that she'd throw me to the wolves any time the pack got too close."

"So you threw her instead?"

"If you want to put it that way, yes," Mason admitted, and took his hand from her shoulder.

She got up and walked toward the outer office.

"Carl Griffin is out there," she said, "and Arthur Atwood, his lawyer."

"Send them in," Mason told her in a flat, dispirited tone of voice.

She opened the door to the outer office, held it open and beckoned to the two men.

Carl Griffin's face showed traces of his dissipation, but he was perfectly poised, very suave, and very much of the gentleman. He bowed his apologies to Della Street for walking in front of her as he passed through the door,

172

smiled courteously and meaninglessly at Perry Mason, as he said, "Good afternoon."

Arthur Atwood was a man in his late forties, with a face that needed sunlight. His eyes were sparkling, but shifty. His head was bald from the forehead to the top where a fringe of hair ran around and down to his ears, making a fuzzy halo for the back of the head. His lips were twisted into a perpetual, professional smile, which was utterly meaningless. The face had taken on lines from that smile, deep calipers running from the nose to the corners of the mouth, with crow's-feet radiating out from the eyes. He was a man who was hard to judge, except in one thing—he was a dangerous antagonist.

Perry Mason indicated chairs and Della Street closed the door.

Carl Griffin started talking. "You will pardon me, Mr. Mason, if I seemed to have misunderstood your motives in this case earlier in the game. I understand that it was your clever detective work which is largely responsible for the confession of Mrs. Belter."

Arthur Atwood interposed affably, "Just leave the talking to me if you will, Carl."

Griffin smiled suavely, bowed toward his counsel.

Arthur Atwood hitched a chair up to the desk, sat down, looked at Perry Mason. "All right, counselor, we understand each other, I take it."

"I'm not certain that we do," said Mason.

Atwood's lips twisted in his perpetual smile, but his sparkling eyes showed no trace of humor.

"You're the attorney of record," he said, "for Eva Belter's contest to the probate of the will. Also for her in her application for letters as special administratrix. It would simplify matters *very* much if you would dismiss both the contest, and the application—without prejudice, of course."

"Whom would it simplify matters for?" Mason asked.

Atwood waved his hand in the direction of his client. "Mr. Griffin, of course."

"I'm not representing Griffin," Mason answered curtly.

Atwood's eyes now joined in the smile of his lips.

"That, of course, is true," he said, *at the present time.* However, I may state candidly, that my client has become very much impressed with the rare ability which you have shown in this matter and with the spirit of fairness which has characterized you throughout. It is, of course, a painful and embarrassing combination of circumstances all around. It comes very much as a shock to my client. However, there can now be no question as to what happened, and my client, in carrying on the business of the estate, will require plenty of competent counsel, if you understand what I mean."

"Exactly what *do* you mean?" Mason asked.

Atwood sighed.

"Well," he said, "if I must speak frankly, or I might say, crudely, inasmuch as we are all here together, just the three of us, it is quite possible that my client will find that the operation of the publication, *Spicy Bits,* is something which will require very specialized attention. I, of course, will be busy representing the balance of the estate, and he had suggested to me that he might like to secure the services of some competent attorney to advise him, particularly with reference to the publication. In fact, to take over the publication during the period that the estate is in probate."

Atwood ceased speaking, and gazed significantly, with his beady, glittering eyes, at Perry Mason. Then, as Mason said nothing, he went on, "The matter would call for some expenditure of time. You would be well compensated, very well compensated, indeed."

Mason was blunt. "All right," he said. "Why mince matters? What you want me to do is to dismiss the contest all the way along the line and leave Griffin in the saddle. He'll see that I make some money out of it. Is that the proposition?"

Atwood pursed his lips.

"Really, counselor, I would hesitate to commit myself upon so blunt an expression of policy, but, if you will think over the statement that I made, I think you will find that it keeps within the bounds of professional ethics, and yet is sufficiently comprehensive to cover the case."

"To hell with all that hooey," Perry Mason said. "I want a plain understanding. I'll talk plainly even if you won't. You and I are on opposite sides of this fence. You're representing Griffin, and trying to get control of the estate, and keep control of it. I'm representing Mrs. Belter, and I'm going to throw that will out of court. It's a forgery, and you know it."

Atwood's lips continued to smile, but his eyes were cold and hard.

"You can't get away with that," he said. "It doesn't make any difference whether the will's a forgery or not. She destroyed the original will. She admits that in her confession. We can prove the contents of that destroyed will, and take under it."

"All right," said Mason, "that's a lawsuit. You think you can. I think you can't."

"Moreover," said Atwood, "she can't take any of the property because she murdered him. It's against the policy of the law for a person to inherit property from one he or she has murdered regardless of any will or other instrument."

Mason said nothing.

Atwood exchanged glances with his client.

"Do you question that?" he asked of Mason.

"Hell, yes," said Mason, "but I'm not going to argue it with you here. I'll do my arguing when I get in front of a jury. Don't think I was born yesterday. I know what you want. You want to be assured of convicting Eva Belter of first degree murder. You think I can help you show premeditation by giving proof of a motive. If you can convict her of first degree murder she can't take any of the prop-

175

erty. That's the law, a murderer can't inherit. But if she's not convicted of murder, even if *she should be convicted of manslaughter,* she could still inherit. You're after the property and you want to bribe me. It won't work."

"If you persist in this course, counselor, *you* may find *yourself* in front of a jury."

"All right," said Mason, "what's the English translation of that, a threat?"

"You can't keep us out of the saddle," said Atwood. "And when we get in the saddle, we will have several important decisions to make. Some of them may affect your activities."

Perry Mason got to his feet.

"I don't like this business of talking around in circles," he said. "I come out and say what I have to say."

"Well," said Atwood, still speaking suavely, "exactly what do you have to say?"

"No!" snapped Mason, explosively.

Carl Griffin coughed apologetically.

"Gentlemen," he said, "perhaps I might say something which would simplify the situation."

"No," said Atwood, "I'm doing the talking."

Griffin smiled at Mason.

"No hard feelings, counselor," he said, "it's a matter of business."

"*Please,*" said Atwood, his eyes staring steadily at his client.

"Oh, all right," said Griffin.

Mason motioned toward the door. "Well, gentlemen, I guess the conference is over."

Atwood tried again. "If you could only see your way clear to dismissing the applications, counselor, it would save time. As it is, you must admit that we have a perfect case, but we didn't like the time and expense necessary to present it."

Mason stared at him stonily. "Listen," he said, "you

may think you've got a perfect case, but right now *I'm* in the saddle, and I'm going to stay in the saddle."

Atwood lost his temper. "You're not in the saddle firmly enough to stay twenty-four hours!"

"You think not?"

"Permit me to remind you, counselor," Atwood remarked, "that you might be considered an accessory to the murder. The police would doubtless be guided by our wishes in the matter, since my client is now the legal heir."

Mason moved over toward him. "Any time I need you to remind me of where I stand, Atwood, I'll call you up."

"All right," said Atwood, "if you want to be disagreeable about it, we'll play that kind of a game."

"That's fine," Mason told him, "I do want to be disagreeable about it."

Atwood signaled to his client, and both men walked to the door.

Atwood strode through it unhesitatingly, but Carl Griffin paused with his hands on the knob, acting very much as though he had something he wanted to say.

Mason's manner, however, was not encouraging. Griffin shrugged his shoulders and followed his attorney out of the office.

When they had gone, Della Street came in.

"Did you reach some kind of an agreement with them?" she asked.

He shook his head.

"Can't they beat us?" she asked, avoiding his eyes.

He seemed to have aged ten years. "Listen, Della, I'm fighting for time. If they'd given me a little time, and some elbow room, I'd have worked this situation out all right. But that woman had to go and drag me into it in order to get herself out. That left me with only one alternative—to get her in so that I could be on the outside, where I could do some good."

"You don't need to explain, chief," she told him. "I'm sorry if I seemed to criticize you. It was all so unexpected, and so totally unlike you, that it surprised me. That was all. Please forget it." But her eyes still avoided his.

"Sure," he said. "I'm going down to Paul Drake's office. You can reach me there if it's anything important, but don't tell anybody where I am."

17

PAUL DRAKE SAT AT A BATTERED DESK IN A CUBBYHOLE of an office and grinned across at Perry Mason.

"Pretty clever work," he said. "Did you have that up your sleeve all the time, or did you just pull it on her when the going got rough?"

Mason's eyes were heavy. "I've had an idea what happened, but getting an idea and getting proof are two different things. Now I've got to save her."

"Forget it," said Drake. "In the first place she isn't worth it, and in the second place, you can't. Her only chance is self-defense and that won't work because she admits he was across the room from her when she shot."

"No," said Mason. "She's a client. I stay by my clients. She forced my hand, and I had to make the play I did. Otherwise, we'd both have been in a mess."

"I wouldn't give her any consideration whatever," Drake said. "She's just a two-timing little tart that saw a chance to marry money, did it, and has been giving everybody the double-cross ever since. You can talk all you want to about your duty to a client, but when the client starts framing a murder rap on you, that's different."

Mason surveyed the detective with heavy eyes. "That's neither here nor there. I'm going to save her."

"How can you?"

"Get this straight," said Perry Mason. "She isn't guilty of anything until she's convicted."

"She confessed," said Drake.

"That doesn't make any difference. The confession is evidence that can be used in the case against her, that's all."

"Well," said Drake, "what's a jury going to do? You'd have to save her on the ground of insanity or self-defense. And she hates your guts. She'll get another lawyer now."

"That's just the point," said Mason. "There might be any one of several different methods now. I'm talking about results. I want you to get everything you can on that Veitch family from the present time, back to the year One."

"You mean the housekeeper?" asked Drake.

"I mean the housekeeper and the daughter. The whole family."

"You still think that housekeeper is keeping something back?"

"I know it."

"Okay, I'll turn the men loose on the housekeeper. How did that Georgia stuff suit you?"

"Swell."

"What do you want me to find out about the housekeeper?"

"Everything you can. And about the daughter too. Don't overlook a single bet."

"Listen," said Drake. "Have you got something up your sleeve, Perry?"

"I'm going to get her out."

"Do you know how you're going to do it?"

"I've got an idea. If I hadn't had an idea how I could get her out, I wouldn't have got her in, in the first place."

"Not even when she tried to put a murder rap on you?" asked Drake, curiously.

"Not even when she tried to put a murder rap on me," said Mason, doggedly.

"You sure as hell do stick up for your clients," said Drake.

"I wish I could convince some other people of that," the lawyer said, wearily.

Drake looked at him sharply. Perry Mason went on, "That's my creed in life, Paul. I'm a lawyer. I take people who are in trouble, and I try to get them out of trouble. I'm not presenting the people's side of the case, I'm only presenting the defendant's side. The District Attorney represents the people, and he makes the strongest kind of a case he can. It's my duty to make the strongest kind of a case I can on the other side, and then it's up to the jury to decide. That's the way we get justice. If the District Attorney would be fair, then I could be fair. But the District Attorney uses everything he can in order to get a conviction. I use everything I can in order to get an acquittal. It's like two teams playing football. One of them tries to go in one direction just as hard as it can, and the other tries to go in the other direction just as hard as it can.

"It's sort of an obsession with me to do the best I can for a client. My clients are entitled to the best I can do for them. It's not my job to determine whether or not they are guilty. That's for the jury to determine."

"Are you going to try and prove this woman was crazy?" the detective asked.

Mason shrugged his shoulders. "I'm going to keep a jury from convicting her," he said.

"You'll never get away from that confession," said Drake. "It shows murder."

"Confession or no confession, they can't prove her guilty of anything, until the jury says she's guilty."

Drake shrugged expressive shoulders, and said, "Oh,

well, there's no use of our arguing about it. I'll turn the men loose on the Veitches, and get all the dope for you."

"I don't suppose I need to tell you," said Mason, "that minutes are precious. All that I've been fighting for all the way along is time enough to get the evidence I want. You've got to work fast. It's a matter of time, that's all."

Perry Mason went back to his office. The puffs under the eyes, which came from fatigue, were more pronounced, but his eyes were steady and hard.

He opened the door of his office. Della Street was at the typewriter. She glanced up, then looked back at her work.

Mason slammed the door shut behind him, walked over to her. "For God's sake, Della," he pleaded, "won't you have confidence in me?"

She flashed him a swift glance.

"Of course I've got confidence in you."

"No, you haven't."

"I'm surprised and a little confused, that's all," she said.

He stood surveying her, moody-eyed, hopeless.

"All right," he said, at length. "You get the State Bureau of Vital Statistics on the telephone, and stay on the telephone until you get the information you want. Get somebody at the head of the department if you can. Never mind what it costs. We want the information, and we want it right now. We want to know whether or not Norma Veitch was ever married. My best guess is that she was. And we want to know if there's been a divorce."

Della Street stared at him.

"What's that got to do with the murder case?"

"Never mind," he said. "Veitch is probably her real name. That is, it's her mother's name, and it would be the name that was on the marriage license as the name of the bride when she was married. Of course, she might not have been married, and she might not have been

181

married in this state. But there's something funny about the whole set up. And there's something in her past that she's holding back. I want to know what it is."

"You don't think Norma Veitch was mixed up in it in any way, do you?" Della Street asked.

Mason's eyes were cold, his face determined.

"All I've got to do is to raise a reasonable doubt in the minds of the jury," he told her. "Don't forget that. Get on the telephone and get that information."

He walked into his inner office and closed the door. He started pacing back and forth, his thumbs propped in the armholes of his vest, his head bowed in concentration.

He was still pacing the floor, half an hour later, when Della Street opened the door.

"You were right," she said.

"How?"

"She was married. I got the dope from the Bureau of Vital Statistics. She was married six months ago to a man named Harry Loring. There's no record of a divorce."

Perry Mason gained the door with three quick strides, pushed it impatiently to one side, strode across the outer office, and went at almost a run down the corridor to the stairs. He took the stairs down to the floor on which Paul Drake had his office and banged on the exit door of Drake's office with impatient fists.

Paul Drake opened the door.

"Hell, it's you! Don't you ever stay in your office to see clients?"

"Listen," Mason told him, "I've got a break. Norma Veitch was married!"

"What of it?" asked Drake.

"She's engaged to Carl Griffin."

"Well, couldn't she have gotten a divorce?"

"No. There's no divorce. There wasn't time for a divorce. The marriage was only six months ago."

"Okay," said Drake. "What do you want?"

"I want you to find her husband. His name's Harry Loring. I want to find out when they separated, and why. And I'm particularly anxious to find out whether she ever knew Carl Griffin before she came to the house on her visit. In other words, I want to know whether she'd ever visited her mother while her mother was working at Belter's place, before the date of this last visit."

The detective whistled.

"By God!" he said. "I believe you're going to set up a defense of emotional insanity, and the unwritten law for Eva Belter."

"Will you get busy on that thing right away?"

"I can have it for you inside of half an hour if he's anywheres in the city," said Drake.

"The sooner the quicker. I'll be waiting in the office."

He went back to his own office, walked past Della Street without a word.

She stopped him as he was entering his office. "Harrison Burke telephoned."

Mason raised his eyebrows.

"Where is he?"

"He wouldn't say. He said he was going to call later. He wouldn't even leave me a telephone number."

"Presume he's read about the new development, in the extras," said Mason.

"He didn't say. Just said that he'd call later."

The telephone rang.

She motioned toward the inner office.

"This is probably the call," she said.

Mason went into the inner office.

He heard Della Street say, "Just a moment, Mr. Burke," and then as he took down the receiver, Burke's voice on the wire:

"Hello, Burke," he said.

Burke's voice was still impressively resonant, but there was an over-tone of panic in it. Every once in a while it seemed that his voice would climb to the high notes and crack, but he always managed to get it back after just the one break.

"Listen," he said, "this is awful. I've just read the papers."

Mason said, "It's not so bad. You're out of the murder case. You can pose as a friend of the family on the other. It isn't going to be pleasant, but it isn't like being held for murder."

"But they'll use it against me in my campaign."

"Use what?" Mason inquired.

"My friendship with this woman."

"*I* can't help that," Mason told him, "but I'm working on an out for you. The District Attorney isn't going to let your name get mixed into the case unless he has to show a motive at the trial."

Burke's voice became more orotund.

"That," he said, "was what I wanted to discuss with you. The District Attorney is very fair. Unless there's a trial my name won't be dragged into it. Now you might fix things so there wouldn't be a trial."

"How?" Mason asked.

"You could persuade her to plead guilty to second degree murder. You're still acting as her attorney. The District Attorney would let you see her—on that understanding. I've talked with him."

Mason snapped a swift reply. "Nothing doing!" he said. "I'm going to try to protect your interests, but I'll do it my way. You keep under cover for a while."

"There'd be a nice fee," said Harrison Burke in a suave, oily voice, "five thousand in cash. Perhaps we could even make it a little more. . . ."

Perry Mason slammed the receiver back on its hook.

The lawyer resumed his pacing of the floor. Fifteen or twenty minutes later the telephone rang.

Mason took down the receiver and heard Paul Drake's voice. "I think we've got your man located. There's a man named Harry Loring who is at the Belvedere Apartments. His wife left him about a week ago and is said to have gone to live with her mother. Do we want him?"

"You bet we want him," Mason said, "and we want him quick! Can you go out there with me? I'll probably want a witness."

"Okay," Drake said. "I've got a car here if you haven't."

"We'll take two cars. We may need them."

18

HARRY LORING WAS A THIN, NERVOUS INDIVIDUAL, WITH a habit of blinking his eyes rapidly, and moistening his lips nervously with the tip of his tongue. He sat on a trunk which was strapped and shook his head at Paul Drake.

"No," he said, "you've got the wrong party. I'm not married."

Drake looked at Perry Mason. Mason gave a faint shrug to his shoulders, which Drake interpreted as a signal to him to do the talking.

"Did you ever know a Norma Veitch?" he asked.

"Never," said Loring, darting his tongue to his lips.

"You're moving out?" asked Drake.

"Yes," Loring said. "I can't keep on with the rent here."

"Never been married, eh?"

"No, I'm a bachelor."

185

"Where are you moving?"

"I'm sure I don't know—yet."

Loring looked from face to face with his eyes blinking.

"Are you gentlemen officers?" he asked.

"Never mind about us," said Drake. "We're talking about you."

Loring said, "Yes, sir," and lapsed into silence.

Drake flashed Mason another glance.

"Packing up rather suddenly, aren't you?" Drake went on.

Loring shrugged. "I don't know as it's sudden. There isn't much to pack."

"Now listen," Drake said, "there's no use for you to try to string us along, because we can check up on you and find out the facts. You say you have never been married. It that right?"

"Yes, sir. I'm a bachelor, just like I told you."

"Okay. Now the neighbors say you were married. There was a woman here who lived in the apartment with you, as your wife, up until about a week ago."

Loring's eyes blinked rapidly. He shifted his position on the trunk, nervously.

"I wasn't married to her," he said.

"How long have you known her?"

"About two weeks. She was a waitress at a restaurant."

"What restaurant?"

"I've forgotten the name."

"What was her name?"

"She went under the name of Mrs. Loring."

"I know that. What was her real name?"

Loring paused and darted his tongue to his lips. His eyes fidgeted uncertainly about the room.

"Jones," he said, "Mary Jones."

Drake laughed sarcastically.

Loring said nothing.

"Where is she now?" asked Drake, suddenly.

186

"I don't know. She left me. I think she went away with somebody else. We had a fight."

"What was the fight about?"

"Oh, I don't know. It was just a fight."

Drake looked over at Mason once more.

Mason stepped forward and took the conversational lead.

"Do you read the papers?" he said.

"Once in a while," said Loring, "not very often. Sometimes I look at the headlines. I'm not very much interested in newspapers."

Mason reached to his inside pocket, and took out some of the clippings from the morning newspaper. He unfolded one which showed a picture of Norma Veitch.

"Is that the woman that was here with you?" he asked.

Loring barely glanced at the photograph, but he shook his head emphatically.

"No," he said, "that wasn't the woman."

"You haven't even looked at the picture yet. You'd better look at it before you get too positive in your denials."

He thrust the picture in front of Loring's eyes. Loring took the clipping and studied the picture for some ten or fifteen seconds.

"No," he said, "that isn't the woman."

"Took you quite a while this time to make up your mind, didn't it?" Mason pointed out.

Loring said nothing.

Mason suddenly turned and nodded to Drake.

"All right," he said to Loring, "if that's the attitude you want to take, you'll have to take your medicine. You can't expect us to protect you if you're going to lie to us."

"I'm not lying."

"Come on, Drake. Let's go," Mason said, grimly.

The two men walked from the apartment, and closed

187

the door behind them. In the corridor, Drake said: "What do you make of him?"

"He's a rat or he'd have tried the stunt of becoming indignant, and asking us what the hell we meant by inquiring into his business. He looked to me as though he'd been on the dodge sometime in his life, and he's afraid of the law. He's used to being bullied by detectives."

"About the way I've got him sized up," said Drake. "What are we going to do?"

"Well," said Mason, "we can take this picture and see if we can find some of the neighbors in the apartment who can identify her."

"The newspaper picture isn't so very good. I wonder if we can't get a photograph," Drake said.

"We're working against time," Mason reminded him. "Something may break in this thing almost any minute, and I want to keep ahead of the game."

"We didn't get very rough with him," Drake pointed out. "He's the kind of a man who would cave in if we went after him, hammer and tongs."

"Sure," said Mason. "We'll do that when we get back. I want to get a little more dope on him if I can. I think he'll turn yellow as soon as we put a little pressure on him."

Steps sounded on the stairs.

"Wait a minute," said Drake, "this looks like somebody coming."

A thick-set man, with heavy shoulders, plodded patiently up the stairs and into the corridor. His clothes were shiny, and his cuffs were frayed. Yet there was an air of determination about him.

"Process server," whispered Mason to Drake.

The man came toward them. His manner was that of one who had, at one time, been a peace officer, and still retained something of the bearing of an officer.

He looked at the two men and said, "Are either of you Harry Loring?"

Mason promptly stepped forward.

"Yes," he said, "I'm Loring."

The man reached in his pocket.

"I guess," he said, "you know what this is about. I have here a summons and a copy of a complaint, and copy of summons in the case of Norma Loring versus Harry Loring. I hereby show you the original summons, and deliver to you a copy of the summons and the complaint."

He smiled wanly.

"I guess you know what it's all about. I understood it was a case that wasn't going to be contested and you were expecting me."

Mason took the papers.

"Sure," he said, "that's all right."

"No hard feelings," said the process server.

"No hard feelings," said Mason.

The process server turned, made a notation on the back of the original summons in pencil, and walked slowly and methodically to the stairs. As he went down, Mason turned to Drake and grinned.

"A break," he said.

The two men unfolded the copy of the complaint.

"It's an action for an annulment instead of a divorce," said Mason.

They read down the allegations of the complaint.

"That's the date of the marriage, all right," said Mason. "Let's go back."

They pounded on the panels of the door to the apartment.

Loring's voice sounded from the inside.

"Who is it?" he asked.

"Papers to be served on you," said Mason.

Loring opened the door and recoiled as he saw the two men standing there.

"You!" he exclaimed. "I thought you'd gone."

Mason pushed his shoulder against the door, and walked into the apartment. Drake followed him.

Mason held out the papers which he had taken from the process server.

"Listen," he said. "There's something funny. We had these papers to serve on you, and understood that you knew all about it. But before we could serve them, we had to make certain that we were serving the right party, so we asked you the questions about your marriage, and..."

Loring said, eagerly, "Oh, *that's* it, is it? Why didn't you say so? Sure, that's what I was waiting for. They told me to wait here until the papers came, and then to get out just as soon as they were served on me."

Mason gave an exclamation of disgust. "Well, why the hell didn't you say so instead of putting us to all this trouble? Your name is Harry Loring, and you married Norma Veitch on the date mentioned in this complaint. Is that right?"

Loring leaned forward to look at the date mentioned in the complaint.

Mason indicated it with his right forefinger.

Loring nodded his head. "That's right."

"And you separated on this date. It that right?" said Mason, moving his forefinger down to the next date.

"That's right."

"All right," said Mason; "this complaint says that at the time you were married, you had another wife living, from whom you had not been divorced, and that therefore the marriage was illegal, and that the plaintiff wants to have the marriage annulled."

Again Loring nodded.

"Now listen," said Mason, "that's not right, is it?"

Loring nodded.

"Yes, sir," he said, "that's the ground she's getting the marriage set aside on. That's right."

190

Mason asked, "Is it true?"

"Of course it's true."

"Then it becomes my duty to arrest you for bigamy." Loring's face blanched.

"He said there wouldn't be any trouble," said Loring.

"Who said that?" asked Mason.

"The lawyer that called on me. Norma's lawyer."

"Just stringing you along," Mason declared, "so that they can get the marriage set aside and Norma could marry this fellow who's heir to a couple of million dollars."

"That's what they said, but they said there wouldn't be any trouble, that it was just a formality."

"Formality be damned!" Mason told him. "Don't you know there's a law against bigamy?"

"But I wasn't guilty of bigamy!" protested Loring.

"Oh, yes, you were," said Mason. "Here it is set forth in black and white, over the signature of the lawyer, and the oath of Norma. It says right here that you had another wife living at the time of the marriage, and that you were never divorced from her. Therefore, we've got to ask you to go to Police Headquarters with us. I'm afraid you've got in serious trouble over this thing."

Loring become nervous.

"It isn't true," he said, finally.

"How do you mean it isn't true?"

"I mean that it isn't true. I mean I was never married before. Norma knows that! The lawyer knows that! I talked with them and they said that they couldn't wait to get a divorce, because that would take a long time, but that Norma had a chance to marry this man and that I would get a piece of change out of it if I let Norma go ahead and file this action. Then I was to file some kind of an answer in which I admitted that I had had another wife living, but claimed that I thought that I was divorced at the time of the marriage. They

191

said that that would keep me in the clear, but it would fix things so she could get the marriage annulled. The lawyer had an answer of that kind already fixed up, and I signed it. He's going to file it tomorrow."

"And then rush the annulment through, eh?" asked Mason.

Loring nodded.

"Well," said Mason, "it doesn't ever pay to try and lie to people who are trying to get the facts of the case. Why didn't you tell me that in the first place and save all this trouble?"

"The lawyer told me not to," said Loring.

"Well, he was crazy," Mason said, "we've got to make a report on the thing. So you'd better give us a written statement to that effect, and then we can turn it in when we make our report."

Loring hesitated.

"Or else," suggested Mason, "you can come on down to Headquarters and explain it down there."

Loring said, "No, no. I'll give you the statement."

"Okay," Mason said, and took a notebook and fountain pen from his pocket. "Sit down there on the trunk," he said, "and write out the statement. Make it complete all the way along the line. Say that you never had another wife, that the lawyer explained to you that he wanted Norma to get a quick annulment, and that he fixed it up that you were to say you had another wife living so that Norma could marry this chap that's going to inherit the fortune."

"That won't get me in any trouble then?"

"That's the only way you can keep out of trouble," said Mason. "There's no use of my explaining it to you, but you almost got yourself in a pretty serious mess. It's a good thing you came clean with us. We were just planning to take you down to Headquarters."

Loring sighed. "All right," he said, and took the fountain pen. He sat down and began a laborious scrawl. Mason stood and watched him, feet planted wide apart, eyes steady and patient. Drake grinned and lit a cigarette.

It took Loring five minutes to make the statement. Then he passed it over to Mason. "Will this do all right?" he asked. "I'm not much good at this sort of stuff."

Mason took the statement and read it.

"That's fine," he said, "sign it."

Loring signed it.

"All right," said Mason. "Now the lawyer wanted you to get out of here, didn't he?"

"Yes. He gave me money and told me that I mustn't be here. He didn't want me to be where I could be interviewed if anybody should try to find me."

"That's fine," Mason told him. "Do you know where you are going?"

"Some hotel," said Loring. "It didn't make any difference which hotel."

"Okay," Drake said. "You come along with us, and we'll get you a room. You'd better get it under some other name so that you won't be bothered in case anybody should try to look you up. But you've got to keep in touch with us. Otherwise there might be some trouble. We may have to ask you to verify this written statement in the presence of some witness."

Loring nodded.

"The lawyer should have told me about you fellows," he said. "He might have got me into an awful mess."

"He certainly should have," Mason agreed. "You might have been on your way to Police Headquarters by this time, and it wouldn't have gone easy with you, once you'd got there."

"Did Norma come up here with the lawyer?" Drake asked.

"No," said Loring, "her mother came first. And then the lawyer came."

"You didn't see Norma?"

"No, just her mother."

"All right," Mason told him. "You come with us, and we'll take you to the hotel we want you to stay at, and get you a room. You'd better go under the name of Harry LeGrande."

"How about the baggage?" asked Loring.

"We'll take care of the baggage. We'll send the transfer man after it. The hotel porter will take care of everything for you. All you've got to do is to go over there. We've got a car waiting, and you'd better go over with us right now."

Loring wet his lips. "Believe me, gentlemen, this is a relief. I was nervous, sitting there waiting for the man to come with the papers. I got to wondering afterwards if that lawyer knew everything he was doing."

"He was all right," Mason commented, "but he just forgot to tell you a couple of things. He probably was in a hurry, and excited."

"Yes," Loring admitted, "he seemed excited all right."

They took him down to the car, and Mason said, "We'll go to the Hotel Ripley, Drake. It's conveniently located."

Drake said, "Yeah, I understand."

They drove in silence to the Hotel Ripley, where Mason was registered under the name of Johnson. He approached the clerk and said, "This is Mr. LeGrande from Detroit, my home town. He wants to get a room here for a few days. I wonder if you can give him one on the same floor that I have?"

The clerk consulted a card index. "Let's see. You're in 518, Mr. Johnson?"

"That's right," Mason said.

"I can give him 522."

"That'll be fine, and there's some baggage to take care of. I'll speak to the porter about it."

They went up to the room with Loring.

"Okay," Mason said to Loring. "Now you stay right here, and don't go out. Be where you can answer the telephone if we should give you a ring. We've got to make a

194

report to Headquarters. Then it may be that they'll want to ask you a couple more questions. But it's going to be all right now that we've got your written statement. You're in the clear."

"That's fine," Loring said. "I'll do just what you say. The lawyer said to communicate with him as soon as I got located. Should I do that?"

"No," said Mason, "that's not necessary, because you've communicated with us. Don't communicate with anybody. Just stay right here and wait until you hear from us. You can't do anything until after we've reported to Headquarters."

"All right," agreed Loring, "whatever you say."

They went out of the room and closed the door.

Drake turned to Mason and grinned.

"Boy, what a break!" he said. "What do we do now?"

Mason strode toward the elevator.

"Now we pull a grandstand," he said.

"Let her go," Drake told him.

Mason stopped in the lobby and called Police Headquarters. He asked for Sidney Drumm in the Detective Bureau. After a minute or two, he heard Drumm's voice on the wire.

"Drumm," he said, "this is Mason. I've got another development in that Belter case, but I've got to have some cooperation on it. I gave you a break on the arrest of the woman, and I want you to give me a break now."

Drumm laughed. "I don't know whether you gave it to me or not. I walked in on it, and you came through to save your own bacon."

"Well, there's no use arguing about it," Mason said. "I gave you the dope, and you got the credit."

"Okay," said Drumm, "what do you want?"

"Round up Sergeant Hoffman and meet me at the foot of Elmwood Drive. I want to go up to Belter's house with you. I think I can show you something there."

"I don't know as I can get the Sergeant. He may have left already," Drumm protested. "It's late."

"If he's left, round him up," Mason told him. "And I want you to have Eva Belter out there."

"Gee," said Drumm, "that's a big order. If we take her out now, it'll attract attention."

"It won't if you sneak her out," said Mason. "Bring along as many men as you want, only don't make any noise about it."

"I don't know how the Sergeant will look at this thing," Drumm protested, "but I don't think there's a chance in a million."

"Well," Mason said, "do the best you can. If he won't bring Eva Belter, get him to come himself. I'd like to have her there, but I've got to have you two."

"Okay," said Drumm. "I'll meet you at the foot of the hill, unless something goes wrong. I can get him to go if he's here."

"No. That won't do. You find out first whether or not you can make the arrangements, and then wait there. I'll call you back in about five minutes. If you can go, I'll meet you at the foot of the hill. If you can't there's no use going on a wild-goose chase."

"Okay, five minutes, then," Drumm said, and hung up.

Drake looked at Mason. "You're biting off a pretty big mouthful there, guy."

"That's all right. I can chew it."

"Do you know what you're doing?"

"I think I do."

"If you're trying to work up a defense for the jane, it would be a whole lot better to work it up without the police being there so that you could spring it on them as a surprise."

"This isn't that kind of a defense," said Mason. "I want the police there."

Drake shrugged his shoulders.

"It's your funeral," he said.

196

Mason nodded, walked over to the cigar counter, and bought some cigarettes. He waited five minutes, and then called Drumm.

Drumm said, "I've got Bill Hoffman sold on the idea, Mason, but he won't take Eva Belter out there. He's afraid you're laying a trap for him. There are two dozen reporters hanging around the jail, and we couldn't move her any place without having that bunch trailing along. Hoffman's afraid you might get him out there, and pull a fast one that the newspapers could play up, and he'd be in a sweet spot. But he's willing to go himself."

"Okay," Mason said, "that may work out just as well. Meet me out at the foot of Elmwood Drive. We'll be waiting there in a Buick coupé."

"Okay," said Drumm. "We're leaving in about five minutes."

"See you later," Mason told him, and slipped the receiver back on its hook.

19

■

THE FOUR MEN PUSHED THEIR WAY UP THE STEPS OF the Belter Mansion.

Sergeant Hoffman frowned at Mason. "Now listen, no funny business. I'm trusting you on this."

"Just keep your eyes and ears open, and if you think I'm uncovering something, go ahead and follow up the lead. Any time you think I'm trying to give you the double-cross, you can walk out."

Hoffman said, "That's fair."

"Let's remember one or two things before we start," cautioned Mason. "I met Mrs. Belter at the drug store down at the foot of the hill. We came up together. She didn't have her keys with her, and she didn't have her purse. She'd left the door unlocked when she came out so she could get back in. She told me that the door was unlocked. When I tried the door it was locked. The night latch was on."

Drumm said, "She's such a liar, that if she told me a door was open, I'd *know* it was locked."

"That's all right, too," Mason said, doggedly insistent, "but remember that she didn't have her keys with her, and she went out in the rain. She was bound to figure on getting back some way."

"Maybe she was too rattled," Hoffman pointed out.

"Not that baby," Mason remarked.

"All right, go on," said Hoffman, interested. "What's next?"

"When I went in," said Mason, "there was an umbrella in the stand, which was wet. There was a pool of water which had drained down from it on the floor underneath. You probably noticed it when you came."

Sergeant Hoffman's eyes narrowed.

"Yes," he said, "come to think of it, I *did* notice it. What about it?"

"Nothing," said Mason, "yet." He reached out his finger and pushed the bell button.

After a few minutes the door was opened by the butler, who stared at them.

"Carl Griffin home?" asked Mason.

The butler shook his head. "No, sir," he said, "he's out. He had a business appointment, sir."

"Mrs. Veitch, the housekeeper's here?"

"Oh, yes, sir, of course, sir."

"And her daughter, Norma?"

"Yes, sir."

"All right," said Mason, "we're going up to Belter's

198

study. Don't say anything to anybody about the fact that we're here. Do you understand?"

"Yes, sir," said the butler.

Hoffman stepped inside the door, and looked searchingly at the hall stand in which the umbrella had stood the night of the murder. His eyes were very thoughtful.

Drumm was whistling nervously in a low, almost inaudible note.

They climbed up the stairs, and went into the suite where Belter's body had been found. Mason switched on the lights and began a minute search of the walls.

"I wish you folks would take a look," he said.

"What are you looking for?" asked Drumm.

"A bullet hole," said Mason.

Sergeant Hoffman grunted and said, "You can save your time on that. We've gone over every inch of these rooms, and had them photographed, and mapped. A bullet couldn't have gone through here without leaving a hole we'd have seen, and there'd have been plaster chipped loose."

"I know," said Mason. "I made a search before you got here, looking for the same thing, and couldn't find it. But I want to make one more search. I know what *must* have happened, but I can't prove it, yet."

Sergeant Hoffman, suddenly suspicious, said, "Look here, Mason! Are you trying to clear that woman?"

Mason turned and faced him.

"I'm trying to show what actually happened," he said.

Hoffman frowned. "That doesn't answer my question. Are you trying to free the woman?"

"Yes."

"That lets me out," said Hoffman.

"No, it doesn't," said Mason. "I'm going to give you an opportunity to get your pictures all over the front pages of the papers."

"That's what I'm afraid of," said Hoffman. "You're clever, Mason. I've looked you up."

"All right, if you've looked me up, you know I never go back on my friends. Sidney Drumm is a friend of mine. I got *him* in on this. If it had been any kind of a frame-up, I'd have got somebody I didn't know."

Sergeant Hoffman admitted grudgingly, "Well, I'm going to stick around a little while, but don't try any funny stuff. I want to know what you're getting at."

Mason stood staring at the bathroom. There were chalk-lines on the floor, marking the position in which the body of George Belter had been found.

Suddenly Mason laughed aloud.

"I'll be damned!"

"What's the joke?" asked Drumm.

Mason turned to Sergeant Hoffman.

"Okay, Sergeant," he said, "I'm ready to go ahead and show you something. Will you send for Mrs. Veitch and her daughter?"

Sergeant Hoffman looked dubious. "What do you want with them?"

Mason said, "I want to ask them some questions."

Hoffman shook his head.

"No," he said, "I don't think I want you to—not until I know more about it."

"This is on the level, Sergeant," Mason insisted. "You sit and listen to the questions. Any time you think I'm getting off the reservation, you can stop me. Hell's fire, man! If I wanted to slip over a fast one, I'd run you in front of a jury and then pull my stuff as a surprise. I certainly wouldn't go out and take the police in on the ground floor of what my defense was going to be."

Sergeant Hoffman thought a minute.

"That's logical," he said. He turned to Drumm. "Go on down and round up the two women, and bring them up here," he said.

Drumm nodded and left the room.

Paul Drake stared at Mason curiously. There was not the faintest trace of expression on Mason's face, nor did he say anything during the few minutes which elapsed after Drumm left the room and the time when shuffling steps were heard outside of the door. Then the door opened, and Drumm bowed the two women into the room.

Mrs. Veitch was as sombre as ever. Her dull black eyes stared incuriously at the men in the room. She walked with her peculiar, long, flat-footed stride.

Norma Veitch wore a tight fitting dress, which accentuated the curves of her figure. She seemed proudly aware of her ability to catch the masculine eye as she stared from face to face, with a half smile on her full lips.

Mason said, "We wanted to ask you a few questions."

Norma Veitch said, "Again?"

"Mrs. Veitch, do you know anything about your daughter's engagement to Carl Griffin?" asked Mason, ignoring Norma's comment.

"I know they're engaged."

"Did you know that there was any romance there?" asked Mason.

"There's usually a romance when people get engaged," she said, in her husky voice.

"I'm not talking about that," he told her. "Please answer my question, Mrs. Veitch. Was there any romance between the pair, that you know of, prior to the time that Norma came here?"

The dark, sunken eyes shifted for a moment toward Norma, then came back to Mason's face.

"No," she said, "not *before* they came here. They got acquainted afterwards."

"Did you know your daughter had been married?" asked Mason.

The eyes stared full in his face without any change of expression.

"No," said the woman wearily, "she hasn't been married."

Mason shifted quickly to Norma.

"How about it, Miss Veitch? Were you ever married?"

"Not yet," she said. "I'm going to be. And I don't see for the life of me how that's connected with the murder of George Belter. If you folks want to ask questions about that, I presume we've got to answer them, but I don't see that that means I have to go into my private affairs."

"How could you marry Carl Griffin when you were already married?" Mason asked.

"I'm not married," Norma Veitch said, "and I don't have to stand for these insulting comments."

"That isn't what Harry Loring says," Mason told her.

The girl's face didn't change expression by so much as the flicker of an eyelash.

"Loring?" she said, in a calmly inquiring tone. "Never heard of the man. Did you ever hear of a man named Loring, Mumsey?"

Mrs. Veitch puckered her forehead. "Not that I can recall, Norma. I'm not very good at remembering names, but I don't know any Loring."

"Perhaps," said Mason, "I can refresh your recollection. He's a man that lived in the Belvedere Apartments. He had apartment 312."

Norma Veitch shook her head hastily, "I'm certain there's some mistake."

Perry Mason pulled the copy of the summons and complaint in the divorce action from his pocket. "Then perhaps you can explain how it happened that you verified this complaint, in which you swore on your oath that you had gone through a marriage ceremony with Harry Loring."

Norma Veitch flashed one quick glance at the paper, then shifted her eyes to her mother. Mrs. Veitch's face was quite expressionless.

Norma spoke rapidly.

"I'm sorry that you found that out, but since you did, I may as well tell you. I didn't want Carl to know any-

202

thing about it. I was married and had trouble with my husband and left him. I came here and took my maiden name. Carl met me, and we fell in love with each other at first sight. We didn't dare to do anything about announcing our engagement because we knew that Mr. Belter would be furious. But, after Mr. Belter died, there wasn't any reason why we should keep it secret.

"I found out my husband had another wife living. That's one of the reasons we separated. I talked to a lawyer. He said the marriage wasn't any good. He told me I could get an annulment. I was going to do it quietly. I didn't figure that anybody would know a thing about it or connect the name of Loring with that of Veitch."

"That isn't what Griffin says," Mason told her.

"Of course not," she said. "He doesn't know anything about it."

Mason shook his head.

"No," he said. "You see, Griffin has confessed. We're trying to check up on his confession, trying to find out if you're criminally responsible as an accessory or if you were just the victim of circumstances."

Sergeant Hoffman moved forward. "I think," he said, "that right here is where I'm going to stop the show, Mason."

Mason turned on him. "Listen for one more minute, Sergeant," he pleaded. "You can stop the show then if you want to."

Norma Veitch looked swiftly and nervously from one to the other. Mrs. Veitch's face was a mask of weary resignation.

"What happened," said Mason, "is that Mrs. Belter had an argument with her husband, and fired the shot at him. Then she turned and ran, without waiting to see what had happened. Woman-like, she supposed, of course, that because she had shot *at* a man, she had hit him. As a matter of fact, at that distance, in her excitement, the chances were very strongly against her hitting him.

"She turned and ran down the stairs, grabbed a coat, and went out into the rain. You, Miss Veitch, heard the shot and you got up, dressed, and came to see what the trouble was. In the meantime Carl Griffin had driven up to the house, and had come in. It was raining and he had put his umbrella in the rack, and went upstairs to the study.

"You heard Griffin's voice and Belter's voice, and listened. Belter was telling Griffin about how his wife had shot at him, and that he'd uncovered proof of her infidelity. He mentioned the man's name to his nephew and asked his nephew what should be done about it.

"Griffin became curious as to the shooting, and got Belter to stand in the door of the bathroom, just as he'd been standing when Mrs. Belter shot at him. When Griffin had him in that position, he raised the gun and shot Belter through the heart. Then he put the gun down, ran down the stairs, out through the front door, jumped in his car, and drove away.

"He went out and got himself good and tight, so that he could put up a better front, let the air out of one tire, so as to account for his delay in getting here, and drove up, after he knew the police had arrived. He pretended that it was the first time he'd returned since he went out in the afternoon. But he forgot about his umbrella which was in the hallway, and he overlooked the fact that he'd found the door open when he came in, and had put the night latch on it when he went upstairs.

"He shot his uncle because he knew that he was going to inherit under the will, and he realized that Eva Belter *thought* she had shot him. He knew that the gun could be traced to her and that the evidence was all against her. The purse in which Belter had found the incriminating evidence, which connected her with the man who was trying to keep his name out of the scandal sheet, was in Belter's desk.

"You and your mother talked over what you had seen,

and decided that it was a fine opportunity to make Griffin pay a good price for silence. So it was agreed that he was to have his alternative of being convicted of murder, or making a marriage which would be advantageous to you."

Sergeant Hoffman scratched his head, and looked puzzled.

Norma Veitch flashed a swift glance to her mother.

Mason said slowly, "This is your last chance to come clean. As a matter of fact, you're both accessories after the fact, and, as such, you're liable to prosecution, just as though you were guilty of murder. Griffin has made his statement, and we don't need your testimony. If you want to try to keep up the deception, go ahead. If you want to coöperate with the Police Department, now's your time to do it."

Sergeant Hoffman interrupted. "*I'm* just going to ask you one question," he said, "and that's going to stop this business. Did you, or did you not, do what Mason says, or substantially what he said?"

Norma Veitch said, in a low voice, "Yes."

Mrs. Veitch, roused at last, whirled on her with fury snapping in her eyes.

"Norma!" she screamed. "Shut up, you little fool! It's a bluff! Can't you see?"

Sergeant Hoffman moved toward her. "It may have been a bluff, Mrs. Veitch," he said slowly, "but her statement and your comment have spilled the beans. Go ahead and tell the truth. It's the only thing left for you to do; otherwise I'm going to figure you're accessories after the fact."

Mrs. Veitch ran her tongue along the line of her lips, and burst out furiously, "I should have known better than to trust the little fool! She didn't know anything about it. She was asleep, as sound as a log. *I* was the one who heard the shot and came up here. I should have made him marry *me,* and never taken my daughter into my confidence. But I thought it was a break for her, and I gave it to her. That's the gratitude I get!"

Sergeant Hoffman turned and stared at Perry Mason.

"This," he said, "is a hell of a mess. What happened to the bullet that missed Belter?"

Mason laughed. "Sergeant," he said, "that's what had me fooled all along. That wet umbrella in the rack, and the locked door bothered me. I kept figuring what must have happened, and then I couldn't figure out *how* it could have happened. I've been over this room carefully, looking for a bullet hole. And then I realized that Carl Griffin had sense enough to know that he couldn't have pulled the crime if there had been that bullet hole. Therefore, there was only one thing which could have happened to that bullet. Don't you see?

"Belter had been taking his bath. It's an enormous bath tub, and holds over two feet of water when the bath water is drawn. He was furious with his wife and was waiting for her to come in. He heard her come in when he was in his bath, and jumped up and flung on a bathrobe, yelling for her to come up.

"They had their fight, and she shot at him. He was standing in the door of the bathroom, just about where the body was subsequently found. You can stand over there by the door and figure the line of fire by pointing your finger. When the bullet missed him, it went into the bath tub, and the water stopped the force of the bullet.

"Then Carl Griffin came home, and Belter told him what had happened. That's when he unwittingly signed his own death warrant. Griffin saw his opportunity. He got Belter to stand in just the position he had been when the shot was fired, and then Griffin picked up the gun in his gloved hand, pointed it at Belter, fired one shot through the heart, picked up the second empty shell, which had been ejected, put in his pocket, dropped the gun and walked out. That was all there was to it. It was that simple."

MORNING SUN STREAMED THROUGH THE WINDOWS OF Perry Mason's office. He sat at his desk, his eyes bloodshot from lack of sleep, looking across at Paul Drake.

"Well," said Paul Drake, "I got the low-down on it."

"Shoot," Perry Mason told him.

"He caved in about six o'clock this morning," the detective said. "They worked on him all night. Norma Veitch tried to go back on her story when she saw that he was going to sit tight. It was the housekeeper that broke him down. She's peculiar. She would have hung out until the end of the world if her daughter hadn't cracked and spilled the beans."

"So she worked against Griffin finally, eh?" asked the lawyer.

"Yes, that's the funny part of it. She is all wrapped up in the daughter. When she thought there was a chance to make a good alliance for the daughter, she did it. Then, when she realized that Griffin was in a trap and that there was nothing to be gained by sticking up for him, and that the daughter might go to jail as an accessory if she kept on lying, the woman turned her testimony against Griffin. After all, she was the one that knew the facts."

"How about Eva Belter?" asked Mason. "I've got a writ of habeas corpus out for her."

"You won't need it. I think they turned her loose about seven o'clock. Do you suppose she'll come here?"

Mason shrugged his shoulders. "Perhaps she'll be grateful," he said, "perhaps not. The last time I saw her she was cursing me."

The door in the outer office made a sound as it opened, then clicked back into place.

"Thought that door was locked," said Paul Drake.

"Maybe it's the janitor," said Mason.

Drake got to his feet, gained the door of the private office in three swift strides, jerked the door open, looked out, and grinned. "Hello, Miss Street," he said.

Della Street's voice came through from the outer office. "Good morning, Mr. Drake. Is Mr. Mason in there?"

"Yes," said Drake, and closed the door.

He looked at his wristwatch and then at the lawyer. "Your secretary comes to work early," he said.

"What time is it?"

"Not eight o'clock yet."

"She's not due until nine," Mason said. "I didn't want to bother her. She's had so much work piled on her in this case. So I worked out the application for a writ of habeas corpus on the typewriter myself. I got a judge to sign it about midnight, and had it served."

"Well, they turned her loose," the detective said. "You wouldn't have needed the writ."

"It's better to have them when you don't need them than to need them when you haven't got them," Perry Mason said grimly.

Once more the outer door opened and closed. In the quiet of the building the sound came through to the inner office. They heard a masculine voice; then the telephone on Mason's desk rang. Mason scooped the receiver to his ear, and Della Street's voice said, "Mr. Harrison Burke is out here and wants to see you at once. He says it's important."

The business street below the office had not yet taken on its rumble of sounds, and the words were audible to the detective. He got to his feet. "I'm on my way, Perry,"

208

he said. "Just dropped in to tell you that Griffin has confessed and that they've turned your client loose."

"Thanks for the information, Paul," the lawyer remarked, then indicated a door which led to the corridor. "You can go out that way, Paul."

The detective went through the door as Perry Mason said to the telephone, "Send him in, Della. Drake is leaving."

A moment after Mason had hung up the telephone the door opened, and Harrison Burke came into the room. His face was wreathed in smiles.

"Wonderful detective work, Mr. Mason," he said. "Simply wonderful. The papers are full of it. They predicted that Griffin would confess before noon today."

"He confessed early this morning," Mason said. "Sit down."

Harrison Burke fidgeted, moved over to a chair, and sat down.

"The District Attorney," he said, "is very friendly to me. My name is not being released to the press. The only newspaper which knows the facts is that scandal sheet."

"You mean *Spicy Bits?*" asked Mason.

"Yes."

"All right, what about it?"

"I want you to be sure that my name is kept out of that paper."

"You'd better see Eva Belter," the lawyer told him. "She's going to be handling the estate."

"How about the will?"

"The will doesn't make any difference. Under the laws of this state a person can't inherit, under a will or otherwise, from one who has been murdered by his own hand. Eva Belter might not have been able to make her claim to the estate stand up. She was disinherited under George Belter's will. But because Griffin can't take under that will, the property will be returned to the estate, and Eva

Belter will take, not under the will, but as a wife, being the sole surviving heir at law."

"Then she will be in control of the paper?"

"Yes."

"I see," said Harrison Burke, putting his fingertips together. "Do you know what the police are doing about her? I understand she was in custody."

"She was released almost an hour ago," the lawyer said.

Harrison Burke looked at the telephone. "May I use your telephone, counselor?"

Mason shoved it across the desk to him.

"Just tell my secretary what number you want," said the attorney.

Harrison Burke nodded, held the receiver with that air of calm dignity which made it seem that he was posing for a photograph. He gave Della Street a number, then waited patiently. After a moment the receiver made squawking sounds, and Harrison Burke said, "Is Mrs. Belter there?"

The receiver made noise again.

Harrison Burke's voice was oily in its unctuous modulations. "When she comes in," he said, "would you mind telling her that the person who was to let her know when the shoes that she ordered came in, telephoned, and said that he had her size in stock now, and that she could get them whenever she was ready."

He smiled into the transmitter, nodded his head once or twice as though he had been addressing an invisible audience, replaced the receiver with meticulous precision, and pushed the telephone back across the desk.

"Thank you, counselor," he said. "I am more deeply grateful to you than I can well express. My entire career was in jeopardy, and I feel that it was through your efforts that a very grave wrong was averted."

Perry Mason grunted an inarticulate comment.

Harrison Burke stood to his full height, smoothed down his vest, and thrust out his chin.

210

"When one is devoting one's life to public work," he said, in his booming voice, "one naturally makes political enemies who will stoop to any form of trickery in order to achieve their ends. Under the circumstances, any little innocent indiscretion is magnified and held up in the press in a distorted light. I have served the public well and faithfully. . . ."

Perry Mason got to his feet so abruptly that the swivel chair was pushed back until it slammed against the wall.

"You can save that," he said, "for somebody that wants to hear it. As far as I'm concerned Eva Belter is going to pay me five thousand dollars. I am going to suggest to her that about half of this amount should come from you."

Harrison Burke recoiled before the grim savagery of the attorney's tone.

"But, my dear sir," he protested, "My *dear* sir! You weren't representing me. You were merely representing her upon a murder charge, a misunderstanding which might have had the most serious consequences to her. I was involved only incidentally, and as a friend. . . ."

"I'm just telling you," said Perry Mason, "what my advice is going to be to my client. And, as you may remember, she is now the owner of *Spicy Bits*. Whatever *Spicy Bits* publishes or doesn't publish is going to be up to her. I don't think that I need to detain you any longer, Mr. Burke."

Harrison Burke gulped uncomfortably, started to say something, thought better of it, started to hold out his right hand, caught the glint in Perry Mason's eyes, brought the hand to his side, and said, "Oh, yes, of course. Thank you, counselor. I wanted to drop in and express my appreciation."

"Not a bit," said Perry Mason. "Don't mention it, and you can get out to the corridor through that door."

He stood still at his desk, watching the back of the politician as it passed through the door and into the corridor. Then, as the door shut, he stood grimly staring at it, his eyes coldly antagonistic.

The door from the inner office opened softly. Della Street paused in the doorway, watching his profile. Then as she saw that he did not see her, did not even know that she had entered the room, she moved silently across the carpet to his side. There were tears in her eyes as her hands touched his shoulders.

"Please," she said, "I'm so sorry."

He started at the sound of her voice, turned, and looked down into the moist eyes. For several seconds they looked at each other, saying nothing. Her hands clung to his shoulders frantically, as though she were clinging to something that was being pulled from her grasp.

"I should have known better, chief. I read the papers this morning, and felt so low that . . ."

His long arm circled her shoulders, and scooped her to him. His lips pressed down to hers.

"Forget it, kid," he said in gruff tenderness.

"Why didn't you explain?" she asked chokingly.

"It wasn't that," he said slowly, choosing the words, "it was the fact that it needed an explanation that hurt."

"Never, never, never, so long as I live, will I ever doubt you again."

There was a cough in the doorway. Unnoticed, Eva Belter had entered from the outer office.

"Pardon me," she said in icy tones, "if I seem to intrude, but I am very anxious to see Mr. Mason."

Della Street flung herself away from Perry Mason with flaming cheeks, and surveyed Eva Belter with eyes that had lost their tenderness and flashed with rage.

Perry Mason looked at the woman steadily. He seemed not in the least disturbed.

"All right," he told her, "come in and sit down."

"You might," she said, in acid tones, "wipe the lipstick off your mouth."

Perry Mason stared steadily at her.

"That lipstick," he said, "can stay there. What is it you want?"

Her eyes softened, and she moved toward him.

"I wanted to tell you," she said, "how much I misunderstood you, how much it meant to me . . ."

Perry Mason turned to Della Street.

"Della," he said, "open the drawers in those filing cases."

His secretary looked at him with uncomprehending eyes.

Perry Mason pointed to the steel filing cabinets. "Pull open a couple of drawers," he said.

The girl opened the drawers, which were packed with pasteboard jackets that, in turn, were filled with papers.

"Do you see those?" he asked Eva Belter.

Eva Belter looked at him, frowned, and nodded her head.

"All right," said Mason. "Those are cases. Every one of them is a case, and all the other drawers are filled with cases just the same way. They represent cases that I've handled. Most of them are murder cases.

"When I get all done with your case you're going to have a jacket in there, just about the same size as all of the other jackets, and it's going to be of just about the same importance. Miss Street is going to give you a number. Then if anything comes up, and I want to look back at the case to find out what was done, I'll give her that number, and she'll get me the jacket with the papers in it."

Eva Belter frowned.

"What's the matter," she asked, "don't you feel well? What are you trying to do? What do you want to say?"

Della Street stepped from the filing case to the door which led to the outer office. She moved out and softly closed the door. Perry Mason stared steadily at Eva Belter, and said, "I'm just telling you where you stand in this office. You're a case and nothing but a case. There are

213

hundreds of cases in that file, and there are going to be hundreds of other cases. You've paid me some money already, and you're going to pay me five thousand dollars more. If you take my advice you're going to get twenty-five hundred of it from Harrison Burke."

Eva Belter's lip quivered.

"I wanted to thank you," she said. "Believe me, this is sincere. This comes from the heart. I've done play acting with you before, but this time it's real. I feel so deeply grateful to you that I'd do anything on earth for you. You're simply wonderful. I come up here to tell you so, and you start talking to me as though I was just a specimen that had strayed into a laboratory."

This time there were real tears in her eyes, and she looked at him wistfully.

"There's lots to be done yet," he told her. "You've got to see that Griffin is convicted of first degree murder, in order to set that will aside. You've got to keep in the background in this thing, but you've got to keep in the battle. The only money that's available to Griffin is money that's in George Belter's safe. We've got to see that he doesn't get any of it. Those are some of the things that have got to be done. I'm just telling you so you won't think you can get along without me."

"That isn't what I said! That isn't what I meant. That isn't what I thought," she said rapidly.

"All right," he said, "I'm just telling you."

There was a knock at the door, which opened from the outer office.

"Yes?" called Perry Mason.

The door opened and Della Street slipped into the room.

"Can you take another case today?" she asked solicitously, looking at his bloodshot eyes.

He shook his head, as though to shake away some mental fog.

"What kind of case?" he asked.

"I don't know," she said. "It's a girl expensively dressed, good looking. Seems well bred. She's in trouble, but she won't open up."

"Sulky, eh?"

"Sulky?—Well, perhaps I'd call her sort of trapped."

"That's because you like her looks," Mason grinned. "If you didn't you'd call her sulky. What's your hunch, Della? You usually have pretty good hunches on how the cases are going to turn out. Look at the last client."

Della Street looked at Eva Belter, then looked hurriedly away.

"This girl," she said slowly, "is angry inside, all torn up. She's a lady, though, almost too much of a lady. She's like . . . well, maybe she is just sulky."

Perry Mason heaved a great sigh. The savage glint slowly faded from his eyes, and in its place came a look of thoughtful interest. He raised the back of his hand to his mouth, wiped off the lipstick, and smiled at Della Street.

"I'll see her," he said, "just as soon as Mrs. Belter goes out. And," he added, "that will be in a very few minutes."